"Take your clothes off."

Angel jerked to attention. Blinked twice. "What?"

"Take off all your clothes. Now."

Cole stared at her with that usual intensity, his words perfectly clear, uttered in that brisk, cold tone, but she still didn't understand.

"Why do you want me to take off my clothes?" The idea seemed ludicrous, given the current situation.

"Do it."

She jumped at the sound of his voice. She had to get a hold of herself here. "No." She shook her head adamantly. She wasn't taking off her clothes without a good reason. "Not until you tell me why."

"We walked right into a trap. I'm not taking the chance that there's a bug I don't know about. I need to inspect every square inch of your body."

Dear Harlequin Intrigue Reader,

Our romantic suspense lineup this month promises to give you a lot to look forward to this holiday season!

We start off with *Full Exposure*, the second book in Debra Webb's miniseries COLBY AGENCY: INTERNAL AFFAIRS. The ongoing investigation into the agency's security leak heats up as a beautiful single mom becomes a pawn in a ruthless decimation plot. Next up…will wedding bells lead to murder? Find out in *Hijacked Honeymoon*— the fourth book in Susan Kearney's HEROES, INC. series. Then Mallory Kane continues her ULTIMATE AGENTS stories with *A Protected Witness*—an edgy mystery about a vulnerable widow who puts her life in an FBI special agent's hands.

November's ECLIPSE selection is guaranteed to tantalize you to the core! *The Man from Falcon Ridge* is a spellbinding gothic tale about a primitive falcon trainer who swoops to the rescue of a tormented woman. Does she hold the key to a grisly unsolved murder—and his heart? And you'll want to curl up in front of the fire to savor *Christmas Stalking* by Jo Leigh, which pits a sexy Santa-in-disguise against a strong-willed senator's daughter when he takes her into his protective custody. Finally this month, unwrap *Santa Assignment*, an intense mystery by Delores Fossen. The clock is ticking when a desperate father moves heaven and earth to save the woman who could give his toddler son a Christmas miracle.

Enjoy all six!

Sincerely,

Denise O'Sullivan
Senior Editor
Harlequin Intrigue

DEBRA WEBB

FULL EXPOSURE

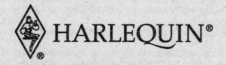

HARLEQUIN®

TORONTO • NEW YORK • LONDON
AMSTERDAM • PARIS • SYDNEY • HAMBURG
STOCKHOLM • ATHENS • TOKYO • MILAN • MADRID
PRAGUE • WARSAW • BUDAPEST • AUCKLAND

ISBN 0-373-22807-4

FULL EXPOSURE

Copyright © 2004 by Debra Webb

ABOUT THE AUTHOR

Debra Webb was born in Scottsboro, Alabama, to parents who taught her that anything is possible if you want it badly enough. When her husband joined the military, they moved to Berlin, Germany, and Debra became a secretary in the commanding general's office. By 1985 they were back in the States, and with the support of her husband and two beautiful daughters, Debra took up writing full-time and in 1998 her dream of writing for Harlequin came true. You can write to Debra with your comments at P.O. Box 64, Huntland, Tennessee 37345 or visit her Web site at www.debrawebb.com to find out exciting news about her next book.

Books by Debra Webb

*Colby Agency
**The Specialists
†Colby Agency: Internal Affairs

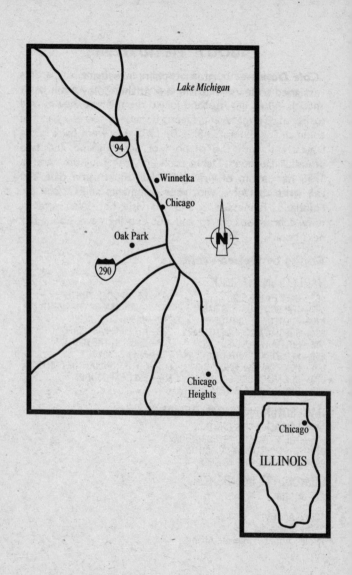

CAST OF CHARACTERS

Cole Danes—An Internal Affairs investigator assigned to ferret out the leak at the Colby Agency. Has he gone too far?

Angel Parker—She is desperate. Someone she loves is in grave danger. Only one man can help her, but will she survive the encounter?

Victoria Colby-Camp—Head of the Colby Agency. She refuses to believe the final report Cole Danes offers.

Lucas Camp—Deputy director of Mission Recovery, and Victoria's loving husband. He will do anything to protect the woman he loves, including going after Danes if he makes a mistake.

Mildred Parker—Victoria's personal assistant. Will her niece, Angel, be able to reach her in time?

Thomas Casey—The director of Mission Recovery, and Lucas's boss. If Lucas can count on anyone for backup, it's Thomas Casey.

John Logan—A specialist at Mission Recovery, and one of Casey's most trusted men.

Keith Anderson—Angel's friend. A man Cole Danes despises for all the wrong reasons.

Errol Leberman—A lifelong nemesis of the Colby Agency. Though Leberman is dead, his evil legacy still taunts Victoria Colby-Camp and her family.

Wyman Clark—The final minion recruited by Errol Leberman. He is in control of this game, and the clock is ticking down.

Chapter One

"Give me one good reason why I shouldn't kill you right now."

The tip of the gun barrel bored into her skull. She shuddered at the harsh words. *Dear God, please help me! Don't let him kill me until I know she's safe.*

"I don't know what else you want from me." The words echoed hollowly from her throat. A defeated sob tore loose from her trembling lips before she could stop it. "I've done everything you asked."

"You're pathetic," the evil man hovering above her hissed. "The least you could have done was fight, but you just dropped to your knees like a spineless puppet." He laughed, the sound cruel, mocking. "Don't you know it's people like you who make the few and strong like us so powerful?" The cold steel drilled harder into her head.

She didn't have to look up to know he stared down at her, the truth in his words glaring like a humiliating spotlight. He would kill her, she didn't doubt her fate for a single moment. And he was right, she was worse than pathetic…less than nothing. She closed her eyes and pictured her sweet baby in her mind. Who would take care of her now? There was no one else.

And it was entirely her own fault.

"Maybe…" the hateful voice offered slowly as the pressure on her skull lessened ever so slightly. "There might be one last use for you."

For the first time since she'd fallen to her knees, pleading for mercy, she looked up at him. "Anything." She moistened her brutally dry lips. "I'll do anything. Just—" she swallowed hard "—just don't hurt her."

"You gave us a name." One side of the man's vile mouth lifted in the barest hint of a smile. "We want him."

Dread expanded in her chest once more. "I don't know what else I can do." She'd done everything they had asked already. He'd promised to leave her alone. But the man who'd made that promise didn't appear to be in charge anymore. Another, even more evil man apparently had control. She couldn't trust this one. Though she'd never met him before today, somehow she knew with complete certainty.

This man would kill her.

She didn't even care anymore. If only he wouldn't hurt—

"Bring him to us," he ordered, a new kind of chill in his tone. "We want him to pay for what he has done."

Confusion spiraled into her already fragmented thoughts. "I—I'm not sure—"

"We want to teach him a lesson first, then he'll pay," he explained, an eerie look of anticipation in those icy gray eyes. "Yes." He nodded succinctly as if having weighed the merit of his suggestion he found it worthy. "Perhaps if you did this for us, we could spare her."

A glint of faltering hope sent a new wave of emotion brimming against her lashes. "Please." She lifted her hands in supplication. "Please don't hurt her." She struggled to draw in an agonizing breath. "I want to help you. I swear I do, just don't—"

"You have forty-eight hours. I'll be in touch with specific instructions. Bring him to us or she dies."

Terror squeezed her heart. "Please." *God, please don't let him do this...* "How can I bring this man to you when I don't even know him? How am I supposed to find him?"

The man wielding the ultimate power of life and death over her world snickered. "Don't worry, Cole Danes will find you."

Chapter Two

Inside the Colby Agency, Monday, 10:30 a.m.

Cole Danes watched Lucas Camp enter the office of Victoria Colby-Camp, head of the Colby Agency. Cole had anticipated this meeting. He'd known when he turned in his final report that his conclusions would not sit well with his employers on this assignment.

No one liked the truth when it hit too close to home.

He'd been summoned to Victoria's office this morning, however, she had insisted on waiting for Lucas's arrival before starting the meeting. Cole hadn't argued. His findings were conclusive. Whether she wanted to believe him or not was strictly her decision. Lucas, however, would surely look upon the situation with a bit more objectivity. He, after all, had been the one to hire Cole. Lucas Camp would not second-guess Cole's work.

Lucas, his trademark limp scarcely noticeable to

anyone unaware of his past, moved to the wing chair adjacent to Cole's and nodded once to his lovely wife as he sat down. He propped his distinctive cane against the chair and leaned back, his full attention settling onto Cole.

"Mr. Danes," Victoria began, her voice stern yet with an underlying fragility that Cole found intensely curious, "I have reviewed your report very thoroughly and I must say that your documentation of evidence is rock solid."

Cole inclined his head in agreement with her assessment. "I'm certain you expected nothing less."

He studied her during the moment of uncomfortable stillness that followed. Strong, capable. Victoria was both of those things. He knew from the dossier he'd compiled upon Lucas's request that he consider this assignment, that she had suffered greatly in her life, had every reason to falter, and yet she had not.

Until now.

The uncertainty—the utter vulnerability—he saw now surprised him. Had his findings somehow served as the final blow that would crumble her already heavily burdened emotional fortress?

"Having recognized that undeniable fact," she continued, surprising him once more with the sudden burst of strength in her tone, "I will, without reservation, stand behind this member of my staff in unconditional rejection of your charges."

Impatience trickled through Cole. His record was irrefutable. He never failed to complete an investigation and his findings were always infallible.

Her denial, he admitted, was not completely unexpected. Though strong and capable, Victoria Colby-Camp operated with one weakness that Cole had long ago conquered, human compassion. A crippling emotion at best.

She cared deeply for her agency and those she employed there. Too deeply, it seemed, to see the truth now.

"I understand your hesitation, Mrs.—"

"No you don't." She leaned forward, braced her arms on her polished mahogany desk. "I've spoken at length with Heath Murphy since his surgery barely thirty-six hours ago. Some of his accusations against you were corroborated by the medical staff at Aspen Valley Hospital. So don't pretend to understand how I feel, Mr. Danes. I'm of the opinion that *feeling* is something you're quite incapable of."

Well, she had him there. He had done what he deemed necessary to complete the mission. He refused to apologize for it.

"Let's not get off track," Lucas offered gently.

Cole turned his attention to the man who'd brought him into this situation. Lucas Camp, deputy director of Mission Recovery, a shadow operation that scarcely anyone was aware of, had hired Cole to perform an internal-affairs investigation to find a leak in the Colby Agency that appeared to go back at least two years.

Victoria and her agency had been plagued by a man named Errol Leberman for nearly two decades. He had kidnapped her son, tortured and brainwashed him, ultimately sending him to assassinate his own mother some eighteen years later. Leberman had spent many of those years, while waiting for the son she thought dead to become the killing machine he needed for his coup de grâce, playing head games with both Victoria and Lucas. There were times when his moves could only have been made with skilled help. And, more recently, with the use of inside information. Lucas had recognized that cold hard fact even when Victoria had not wanted to see it.

One week ago when Cole assumed control of the Colby Agency to begin his internal-affairs investigation he already knew the name of the primary man who had helped Leberman. Cole had needed only two things to complete his work, the identity of the agency employee who had leaked information and the elimination of Leberman's associate.

He had accomplished both. The first he had quickly ascertained through his interrogations and extensive background investigations. The second had taken a bit more time and the help of one of the Colby Agency's investigators. The newest investigator on staff, one who would have no ties to Leberman and the leak. Heath Murphy.

Heath had not failed him, though he had been royally P.O.ed at what he recognized as a setup early in the game. But that was his problem. Cole's single goal was to see that the elimination occurred.

Leberman's associate, Howard Stephens, was dead, and Victoria had her name. The Colby Agency's involvement in the matter was over. Cole had his own agenda from here. Nor would he apologize for using Stephens's own daughter, Jayne, to bring him down.

"Danes," Lucas addressed Cole now, "I brought you into this investigation because you're the best."

He was. Lucas and his team of Specialists were superior, as well. However, Cole had possessed one piece of information they hadn't. That was part of what made him the best in this particular situation. Lucas and his lovely wife had no need to know certain details.

"Thank you, Lucas." Cole looked directly at the man when he spoke, allowed him to visually inspect his eyes and expression. Cole knew he watched for any sign of deceit. "I have yet to fail."

"There's always a first time," Victoria accused.

Cole offered her a patient smile. She responded with a furious glare. "I appreciate that this is a delicate situation, but I can assure you that my assessment is correct."

Lucas held up a hand when she would have argued otherwise. "Let's just say that I agree," he ventured.

Cole knew it was a front to spare his wife from

feeling further injury. Lucas knew he was right. He was no fool, nor was he blinded by overpowering emotion on the subject.

"If you have any doubts," Cole suggested with little attempt to keep the smugness out of his tone, "why don't you speak with the employee yourself? I'm familiar with your interrogation techniques, Lucas, a few questions is all it would take and my conclusion would be corroborated."

Lucas's expression turned hard. "You know the answer to that, Danes."

Oh, yes. He knew why the employee couldn't be questioned. This meeting wasted precious time. Perhaps he was the only one present who truly understood just how little of that valuable commodity remained within grasp.

Mildred Parker, Victoria's longtime secretary and personal assistant. A woman who had started at the Colby Agency with its inception. *She* was the leak. She'd gone missing in action two days ago, at basically the same time the final piece of evidence had confirmed his suspicions.

Victoria stood. Her chair banged against the credenza behind her desk. "I will not listen to another word of this." She glowered at Cole. "Mildred has dedicated her life to this agency. She would never do anything to harm me or anyone else here, much less my son."

She was right about one part. Mildred's involvement in leaked information only went back two years. Prior to that Leberman had used guesswork and an uncanny knowledge of his prey's method of operation to go about his nasty business. No one at the Colby Agency had helped Leberman take the Colby child. He'd merely waited for the right opportunity and utilized a skilled accomplice. Revenge was a strong motivator and as misplaced as his had been, Leberman had been out for the ultimate revenge.

Victoria stormed out of the office. The door slammed, punctuating her determined exit with a firm thwack.

Lucas expelled a heavy breath. "There's more you're not telling me, Danes."

Cole redirected his attention to Lucas. He hadn't expected anything less of the man. Lucas Camp had spent a lifetime reading between the lines. "There is."

"Why haven't you shared this additional information?" Lucas kept his temper carefully contained though Cole knew for a certainty that he felt supremely annoyed by this admission.

"Your wife has no need to know this part," Cole said bluntly. "It would only add to her discomfort." He propped his elbows on the chair's arms and steepled his fingers thoughtfully. "Contrary to popular thinking I do suffer a measure of compassion."

Lucas chuckled but the sound held little humor and his expression exhibited even less. "Perhaps we'll debate that issue another time." The older man's gaze pushed hard against Cole's. "I know you, Danes. You're forty years old. You've spent the past dozen years of your life making other people's lives miserable. You're the best interrogator in the business. Since moving into internal affairs at NSA ten years ago you've proven your ability time and time again. Nothing gets past you. Tell me what it is you're leaving out."

Cole rarely worked directly for the National Security Agency these days. His skills were too highly sought after to remain attached to one agency.

"Fair enough," Cole permitted. But Lucas would only know what he wanted him to know. As good as this longtime superspy was, he wasn't quite as good at deception as Cole.

"If my calculations are correct," he said, choosing his words carefully, "only two men remain of the original group Leberman started some twenty years ago."

Leberman had also been in the military at one time. Trained by a Special Forces type unit, Leberman had left the military on bad terms and then he'd proceeded to start his own little mercenary mini-army. He and Stephens had organized a team of six men, all tops in their field. Together this group, of what Cole considered terrorists, had made a fortune in blood. Kidnappings, assassinations, just to name a couple of their offered services.

Now only two of that original six remained. A

muscle in Cole's jaw ticked despite his efforts to maintain an impassive exterior.

"Go on," Lucas prompted, his expression clearly suspect.

"Those last two want revenge for the elimination of their leader."

"Howard Stephens," Lucas filled in.

Cole nodded. "He basically took over years ago, even before Leberman's death. Leberman was too caught up in revenge against the Colbys to keep up the pace required of a true leader. Though the team still respected him and used him from time to time, he was more a planner than a practitioner."

Lucas shrugged. "No surprise there. I knew Leberman was the brains behind whatever exploits he and his minions executed." He looked directly at Cole once more. "So those last two want you."

"Precisely."

"And you," Lucas added, "believe they're holding Mildred and her niece, Angel, hostage to that end?"

"I do."

That wasn't entirely accurate, but it was close enough. Angel Parker, Mildred's beloved niece, had been the one to actually leak the information. Cole didn't know yet what they'd used against her to get the information. A thorough investigation of her finances had not indicated that she'd done it for money. As a single mother of a three-year-old and a full-time nurse at Winnetka General Hospital, the young woman scarcely eked out a living. Without her aunt's generosity, unmarried and pregnant, Angel likely would have crashed and burned long ago.

Since Mildred had never married or had children of her own and Angel's mother had died years ago, Angel had been like a daughter to Mildred. Angel's child, Mildred's pseudograndchild, wanted for nothing.

"For now," Lucas allowed, "we'll operate under that assumption. Since we haven't been able to contact or locate either Mildred or Angel, my hands are tied to do otherwise. What plan of action do you plan to take?" Lucas cocked an eyebrow. "I, of course, am assuming that you consider this next step part of completing your task here."

Lucas read him rather well even if he slightly missed the mark. Cole couldn't prevent another tiny smile. "Of course."

"Details, Danes," Lucas pressed, his expression as ferocious as a lion protecting his den.

"I will offer myself in trade since it was my investigation that landed Ms. Parker and her niece in harm's way." Cole flared his hands humbly. "I should have anticipated this move but I didn't. As Mrs. Colby-Camp said, perhaps there is a first time for failure even for me."

Lucas didn't look convinced. "I'll call in two of my Specialists to provide backup."

"No," Cole said sharply, allowing his composure

to slip for one fraction of a second before locking down the momentary weakness. "This is something I must do alone. Any outside involvement could trigger an undesirable result."

The level of suspicion in Lucas's gaze increased by several degrees. "Do you have substantiated intelligence to confirm that assessment?"

"All I have is gut instinct." Cole angled his head and surveyed the man analyzing him so closely. "Isn't that the reason you hired me? For my instincts?"

Lucas backed off marginally. "I will expect to be kept up to speed on every step you take. I understood and tolerated your need for secrecy as you conducted this investigation into the employees of this agency. But I will not permit you to proceed under those terms now."

Cole stood. "I'll keep you abreast of the situation."

Lucas pushed to his feet with less effort than one would think considering he wore a prosthesis for a right leg. "See that you do."

Cole nodded once before moving toward the door. Lucas Camp would soon learn that Cole Danes shared only what he needed to share. Not even a man as powerful and experienced as Lucas could intimidate him. No one could.

"Just one thing, Danes," Lucas called to his back.

Cole paused at the door and turned to face him.

Again, he indulged himself and allowed a smile to steal past his careful control. "Don't waste your time, Lucas. I know what I have to do. Nothing you say is going to change my methods."

Lucas smiled then, broadly, openly. "I'm well aware of that, Danes. Well aware." His smile vanished as abruptly as it had appeared. "But know this, if anything you do or say causes harm to come to Mildred Parker or her niece, you will answer to me."

For three beats the two men stood there staring at each other, decades of untold secrets and power over life and death pulsing between them.

"Make no mistake," Lucas went on, "I am fully aware that you're keeping something more from me. We all have our secrets." The depth of knowing in that statement glinted in his eyes. "But if yours hurts someone I care about there won't be anyplace on this planet you can hide."

Cole didn't hesitate. "Understood."

With that said he walked out of the office.

He ignored the angry glances from the agency staff members he encountered in the corridor. They had all seen more than enough of him, would likely never forget his name or face.

Few ever did.

But it was all part of the job he was paid to do.

If it were an easy task anyone could do it. Clearly that was not the case.

In the elegant lobby Victoria Colby-Camp stood

near the receptionist's desk. Despite the devastations of her past she had surrounded herself with the best, both in material possessions and in staff and associates. But she, as well as her loyal staff, were mere humans. The finery glittering about them man-made. Just like eighteen years ago, Victoria Colby-Camp could not stop this bad thing from coming home to her. Errol Leberman had started it, but Cole Danes would finish it. For that reason she would never forget or forgive him.

Their gazes collided as if he'd somehow telegraphed that last thought.

She said nothing.

Cole depressed the call button and waited for the car to arrive on the fourth floor. Her silence made no difference to him one way or another.

Words weren't necessary in any event.

He already understood how she felt. She despised him for shedding light on a dark corner of her existence she'd rather not have seen.

She, too, would never forget his name or his face.

Few ever did.

Chapter Three

Winnetka, Illinois, 1:00 p.m.

Nearly three hours and nothing.

Only forty-five hours left.

Fear crammed into her throat, twisted in her stomach.

Angel Parker hadn't left her living room, afraid she might somehow miss her next instructions. What was she supposed to do now?

She moistened her lips and wrung her shaky hands together. How could she save her aunt if no one told her what to do next?

How long was she expected to wait?

Where would she find Cole Danes?

Think, she commanded. She had to think past the fear and confusion. What had the man said?

Don't worry...Cole Danes will find you.

But he hadn't found her.

Angel pushed up from her sofa and started to pace. Her legs felt weak and rubbery after sitting so long. Or maybe it was the lingering effects of the fear. Fear did that—made you weak. She knew that better than most and still she couldn't slow the terror throbbing through her veins. As a nurse she'd watched otherwise calm and knowledgeable patients suffer near panic attacks when faced with the unknown—some unexpected surgery or medical procedure.

No one wanted to face their mortality. Not even the strongest and most intelligent of the human race.

But it wasn't her own death Angel feared.

Her knees buckled and she grabbed for the nearest wall to catch herself. A wave of emotion washed over her, ushering a sob from her dry throat.

She'd done this.

Her aunt could die and it would be her fault.

Angel sagged against the wall and slid down to the floor, the hurt overwhelming her ability to stay vertical.

She'd done everything they'd asked.

For two years she'd lived in fear. She'd changed her work schedule as well as her route to and from work so often she felt certain her superiors considered her a mental case. She'd moved Mia to a different childcare provider every few months, as well.

And still she'd failed.

For a while she'd even foolishly thought herself free of the evil. She laughed bitterly. They hadn't bothered her in four months.

Not since Victoria Colby had gotten her son back.

It was then that Angel had known the magnitude of her sins.

The man who had come to her two years ago, the one who'd held her baby hostage for twenty-four hours just to prove he could, had worked for another even more sinister man named Leberman. Four months ago Mildred had cried and told Angel how thankful she was that Victoria finally had her son back. She'd told Angel about Leberman's death and all he'd done to the Colbys as well as Lucas Camp. As Mildred related the events of the past two years, each one had tied in with the simple, seemingly innocuous, information Angel had secretly passed along.

Each time that telephone had rung, the caller asking only one question, always something so trivial, the call had preceded some evil Leberman had orchestrated.

She'd wanted so desperately to tell her aunt then and there that she'd done this horrible thing. That she had helped make these terrible, terrible things happen to the Colbys. But she couldn't. They had taken her daughter once and had promised that next time Angel would never see her again. All she had to do was give them the information they asked for from time to time and her baby would remain safe. If she ever let them down or told that she'd been contacted, her child would die. She would never forget the look in the man's eyes—a man whose name she didn't even know.

Tell anyone about this and the little girl dies.

Nothing you or anyone could do will save her. Be-
lieve that if you believe nothing else.

To demonstrate his point he'd taken her to Lincoln
Park in broad daylight. Right before her eyes he'd
killed a homeless man sitting on a park bench and
then he'd simply walked away…with the parting advice that she should run like hell and that she was to
remember his warning.

She had remembered.

And she'd believed. He'd killed a man for no reason without caring who saw him.

He would have taken her baby and killed her just
as easily had Angel not cooperated. This kind of
man feared no one…not the authorities, certainly
not the Colby Agency.

Angel curled her arms around her knees and tried
to stop the quaking that rocked her body.

She would carry the guilt of what she'd done to
Victoria Colby to her grave. For these past few
months she had told herself that she had to put it behind her, that things had worked out despite her part
in Leberman's sinister plans. She'd made a mistake.
She had to get past it. She'd thought it was all over.
Nothing she could do would change what was done
any more than she could resurrect that poor homeless man who'd died to prove some madman's point.

Then one week ago she'd gotten a visit rather
than a call. He'd wanted one thing—another seemingly simple bit of inconsequential information. Just

a name. The name of whoever was conducting an internal-affairs investigation at the Colby Agency.

Angel had agreed to get the information and he'd left. She'd known what she had to do. In those few months of reprieve she'd learned a few things…had wondered at what perhaps she could have done to make all this turn out differently. Armed with that knowledge, she had made a decision. She would not let this bastard use her again. She would tell her aunt everything. But first she had to hide her child.

It had taken her four days to make contact with the right people. An underground community of sorts for abused women and children. These people would protect her child until the danger had passed. They had begged her to go into hiding, as well, but she refused. She had to do the right thing this time, had to make this right as best she could.

Once Mia was safely tucked away by people who had the resources to move her from household to household if need be, she had called her aunt. Night before last Angel had gone to her aunt and told her everything. They had cried together and then they'd decided upon the best way to handle the situation. Angel let her aunt make the final decision. They would see Lucas Camp together. He could take care of the man threatening Angel, her aunt insisted.

But that man had shown up just then. He and one of his henchmen. They'd taken Mildred and her to an empty warehouse. They wanted only one thing, the name. Angel hadn't known…but Mildred had. When the man threatened to kill Angel, Mildred had surrendered and given the name.

Cole Danes.

They'd let Angel go with the warning that if the information proved wrong or if she went to the authorities Mildred would die.

Angel hadn't seen her aunt since.

This morning she had learned why. She had just over forty hours before the woman who'd been more like a second mother than an aunt would be killed if Angel didn't come through.

…*you're pathetic.*

The bastard who'd visited her today was right. She was pathetic. Her aunt's life was on the line and she sat there sobbing like a child.

Angel's fingers balled into fists.

She had to be stronger than this.

Her aunt's life depended upon her.

She thought about her options and in a moment of utter clarity, Angel knew just what she had to do.

Suburban Sportsman, Melrose Park, 2:30 p.m.

ANGEL TIGHTENED HER FINGERS around her purse strap and mustered the courage to approach the clerk behind the counter. She'd surveyed the entire upscale sporting-goods store and selected the youngest male clerk on duty.

"Good afternoon." He smiled widely, his gaze instantly doing a head-to-toe sweep as she approached. "May I help you?"

She prayed the nonbusiness interest she saw in his eyes would help her. Angel produced what she hoped would prove a flirtatious smile. "I hope so." She glanced around quickly to make sure no other customers were nearby. "I need to purchase a handgun."

He looked surprised but swiftly recovered. "O…kay. Follow me."

Angel guessed this guy to be no more than twenty-one or two. Cute. Innocent—something she would never again be.

The clerk paused at a display case. "What size weapon were you thinking about?" he asked, his smile not quite so wide now.

Angel scanned the array of offerings behind the glass. Confusion frayed her already frazzled nerves. She didn't know where to begin. Had never so much as touched a gun.

"Something small?" he suggested in a helpful tone.

She nodded. "Yes."

"Very good."

He started behind the counter but she stopped him with a hand on his arm. "What do I have to do to purchase one?"

She'd startled him again. Angel released his arm and tried to look calm and apologetic regarding her behavior. It wasn't working. She could see the uneasiness in his eyes now. "I'm just a little nervous," she offered.

"Ma'am," he said quietly, his gaze darting around to see if anyone had wandered near, "there's a three-day waiting period. Even if you buy one, you can't take it with you today."

The words sent terror slamming against her rib cage. "But I have to have one today." She poured every ounce of desperation she felt into her expression. Prayed he would see…that he would somehow help her. "Please, if you can help me…"

He looked away a moment, spoke under his breath as if he feared being overheard. "Go to Lake Street on the West Side. Try Tito's Pawnshop."

"I can get one today there?" Hope swelled, pushing away some of the paralyzing fear.

He cast a look side to side again. "Maybe." His gaze settled back on her desperate one. "Probably."

"Thank you." Her voice wavered and tears brimmed. She battled the emotions back down. "Thank you."

He touched her arm when she would have walked away. "Listen, lady." His hesitation sent a new trickle of dread snaking through her veins. "I don't know what kind of trouble you're in, but don't go to Lake Street after dark. Go right now. Get your business done and get out of there. Okay?"

She nodded stiffly and turned away.

"Good luck."

She didn't look back. She had to do this. It was the only way.

Lake Street, Chicago's West Side, 2:30 p.m.

FORTY-THREE HOURS.

She had to hurry.

Angel parked at the curb between two SUVs.

No wonder the clerk had warned her about coming here. Though she'd lived in the Chicago area her whole life she couldn't recall ever having been to this particular street.

Young guys huddled in groups called out their wares to slowly passing motorists. *Rocks, blows, weed!*

Drugs. They were selling drugs right on the street in the middle of the afternoon.

Of course she had known things like this happened in all urban areas, but knowing it and seeing it were two different things. Her protected, suburban life hadn't adequately prepared her for this reality. She'd watched scenes on the news channel, but there'd always been police involved handling the situation. There was no sign of policemen here.

Teens, high-school or college types, cruising slowly down the street in their expensive, late-model sedans and SUVs appeared to be the customers the hawkers called to. Other throngs of what looked like older men huddled on the sidewalk tossing dice.

Angel saw a couple of women sitting on their stoops, their preschoolers at their feet, watching the rawest form of capitalism play out.

Angel shook off the troubling thoughts and focused on her mission. She had to purchase a weapon. She refused to be vulnerable, refused to let these evil bastards rule her life a moment longer. She should have done this long ago. Giving herself grace, she hadn't known then how to protect her daughter. Now she did.

Tito's Pawnshop wasn't very large. A glass door and display window, both clad with iron bars, fronted the store. A beggar sat on the sidewalk beneath the window, a used foam cup in his extended hand.

Angel braced herself and entered the shop. Four men loitered inside, two sitting, two leaning on the counter. All four illustrated the term unsavory to its fullest meaning. She moistened her fiercely dry lips and held on tightly to her purse strap as she forged her way toward the counter at the back of the shop. Display case after display case flanked both sides of the narrow aisle. Shelves stocked with pawned merchandise lined the walls behind the display cases. The place smelled like old shoes and sweaty flesh... or maybe it was the men now eyeing her so closely.

The two men leaning on the counter stepped aside as she approached. Each sized her up and snickered but she didn't make eye contact, kept her attention focused on the man behind the counter.

"You lost, lady?" the shopkeeper asked.

"I need to buy a weapon."

The room burst into laughter.

Angel swallowed hard and fought to keep a grip on her thin composure. "I have money." She pulled the wad of twenties out of her purse. She had withdrawn one thousand dollars from her savings account. Surely that would be enough.

Silence abruptly replaced the laughter.

The guy behind the counter looked a little nervous now. "Put your money away, lady." He held up a hand as if trying to avert disaster.

Angel sucked in a shuddering breath and did as he told her. "I…I just need to buy a gun."

Any sign of uneasiness the man had shown morphed instantly into fury. "I don't know what you're doing in this neighborhood, honey, but take my advice and go home." He leaned intimidatingly nearer. "You don't belong here and you damn sure don't want to be caught on this street after dark." He looked at her purse then back at her face. "Now get out of here. Go buy your firearms on the North Side like the rest of your friends."

Every instinct screamed at her to run like hell, but desperation kept her rooted to the spot.

"Come on, baby," one of the guys on her side of the counter said, moving in close. "Let me walk you to your car."

Angel recoiled. "Stay away from me," she ordered, but the quiver in her voice left the threat hollow.

Another round of laughter broke out.

Anger sizzled inside her, burning away the last of her fear. She glared at the man behind the counter. "I said I needed to buy a gun. I was told you could help me. Now, are you here to do business or what?"

He bracketed his waist with his hands. "Just what the hell are you gonna do with a gun?"

Angel flinched. "I…I need protection."

"Honey, you should of thought of that before you came in here," the guy on her left said as he surveyed her backside.

She pushed as close to the counter as possible and let the shopkeeper see the desperation in her eyes. "Please. I need a gun."

Something in his eyes changed, she couldn't say what, maybe the single shred of decency he possessed made an unexpected appearance. He held up a hand for the others to quiet. Angel's heart beat so hard she felt certain everyone in the shop could hear it.

He jerked his head toward the end of the counter. "This way."

Her pulse tripping, Angel followed the man into a dark room behind the counter. The voice of reason screamed again, warning her to run, but she ignored it.

He flipped a switch and the blink of fluorescent

lighting filled the graveyard-quiet, warehouse-grim space. Boxes in a variety of sizes and stages of deterioration lined the walls. A grimy, cluttered desk held center stage.

The man propped on the edge of the desk and looked at her long and hard before he spoke. "What kind of trouble you in, lady?"

"I can't tell you that," she answered sharply. "Just sell me a gun."

He smirked. "All right. What you looking for?"

She hadn't actually considered what kind of gun. She shrugged. "Something small." Her hand moved down to her shoulder bag. "Something I can carry in my purse."

He shook his head slowly from side to side. "Have you ever even fired a weapon?"

"That's none of your business," she snapped. "Stop wasting my time." The vulnerability in that last statement made her cringe.

He threw his hands up. "Whatever." He retrieved a box and set it on the desk. Inside packing materials surrounded the contents. He dug out a smaller box and opened it.

"This—" he exhibited a small black gun "—is a Smith & Wesson 9mm. It's small, less than seven inches in length, and only weighs about a pound and a half. Very light." He depressed something on the weapon and a cartridge slipped out of the handle. "Eight plus one rounds." He pulled back a mechanism on the top. "That action puts one in the chamber." He flipped a small lever. "That's the safety. Turn it off and you're ready to fire." He offered the weapon to her.

It felt heavy in her hands but not as heavy as she'd expected. The cold of the black metal penetrated her skin.

"Hold it like this." He showed her how to grip the weapon. "Feet wide apart for balance. Look down the barrel here."

She did as he instructed.

"Then squeeze the trigger and that's it."

She looked at him and hoped it would be that simple.

He sighed and scrubbed a hand over his face. "Look, if you've never fired a weapon before take some advice."

Angel nodded expectantly.

"Wait till he's close. The closer your target the less likely you'll miss. Aim for the chest."

She licked her lips and tried to swallow back the bile in her throat. "If I hit him in the chest, that's enough right?"

He lifted one shoulder in an indifferent shrug. "Maybe, depends on if you hit anything important."

Okay, she knew that. She was a nurse for God's sake. "So, technically I could hit him in the chest and miss anything vital and he could still hurt me."

"Technically," he said in a mocking tone, "that's

right. So shoot him more than once. Twice at least. If he keeps moving, shoot him until he stops."

The images his words evoked made her tremble. How could she possibly do this? Her aunt's face loomed large in her mind. Because she had no other choice. She nodded. "Got it. Shoot until he stops moving."

He put the weapon back on safety and retrieved two more cartridges from the box and offered them to her. "When you empty a clip, shove in another one and keep firing if you need to."

"Okay." She chewed her lower lip a second, giving a wave of nausea time to pass, then asked, "How much do I owe you?"

He cocked his head and looked at her with the kind of belligerence she would expect from a man like him. "How much you got?"

"One thousand." Her palms started to sweat as reason tried once more to intrude.

His gaze drifted down her body. She shuddered. Even with a conservative sweater, jeans and a suede coat she felt naked somehow. When his attention settled back on her face she didn't miss the sexual hunger there. She held her ground, didn't run—*had* to do this. Whatever it took.

"Eight hundred," he said flatly, sexual interest clearing from his eyes with one downward swoop of his dark lashes.

She counted out the twenties onto the desk and

shoved the goods she'd purchased into her purse. "Thank you."

He moved in close…so close she could smell the spicy scent of the Mexican food he'd had for lunch. "Just remember," he said, his tone menacing, "if you kill someone with that weapon you didn't get it from me. Got that?"

She nodded jerkily. "You don't have to worry, sir," she assured him, a kind of defeat she'd rather not have exposed in her voice. "If I have to use this, I probably won't live to tell anyone anything."

Confusion cluttered his features and then he laughed. He swore softly. "I can't believe I'm saying this…" He looked directly into her eyes. "Lady, why don't you go to the cops for help?"

"Because they can't help me." It seemed incredible. The system she'd believed in her entire life couldn't help her. For that one instant she suddenly knew how people on this side of the tracks felt—totally alone…desperate to survive. She swallowed back a rush of emotion. "No one can help me."

And then she did the only thing she could.

She drove back to her small cottage in the safe, cozy suburb of Winnetka where nothing bad was ever supposed to happen and waited.

There was nothing else she could do until she received further instructions.

Or until Cole Danes showed up.

The man holding her aunt hostage had assured her

that Cole Danes would find her, but every minute that passed made her more uncertain of that possibility.

Except there was no alternative.

She had no option but to wait.

A framed photograph of her and her daughter together tugged at her heart. She reached for it, held it close to her chest. At least her baby was safe. She had done that right if nothing else.

High-pitched, melodious notes abruptly shattered the silence, sending her pulse into another erratic rhythm.

It took a few moments for her to catch her breath and to allow her heart to slide back down into her chest and start beating normally again.

Her cell phone!

She laid the picture and her gun down then snatched up her purse. The zipper hung and she tugged frantically as another ring chimed. Where the hell was it? Finally her fingers wrapped around the cool metal.

"Hello." The two syllables were more a rush of shaky breath than a word.

"When Danes arrives you follow his lead."

It was him. The man holding her aunt.

"What?" She clutched the phone harder. "He's coming now? How do you know? How is my aunt? Let me speak to her."

"No questions. Just follow my instructions. When he arrives, do exactly as he says. We've set a trap for him."

She nodded then realized he couldn't see her. "All right."

"Don't make any mistakes, Angel," he warned. "Time is running out. Don't think we'll stop with your aunt. You may believe you've hidden your daughter from us, but, trust me, we can find her if we need to."

The connection went dead.

Angel's hand fell to her lap, her fingers automatically depressing the end button and then the two others necessary to lock the keypad. Her gaze drifted down to the photograph on the sofa cushion next to her.

For the first time since this nightmare began she realized the full ramifications of her situation. It didn't matter what she did at this point, she was dead. She and her aunt. Tears welled in her eyes. They were both dead.

The only thing she could hope for was that if they got Danes they wouldn't bother her child. If they had what they wanted and she was dead—of no further use to them—why would they need to harm her child? They wouldn't. Her three-year-old was far too young to remember what the men who'd held her looked like. She was no threat to anyone.

Her baby would be safe then. The people harboring Mia would see to it that she was well cared for if Angel never returned. Her baby would be safe.

She had to do this right.

No mistakes.

She thought of Cole Danes. A man she'd never met. Who might even have a family of his own. But she couldn't think about that.

There was no room for sentiment or sympathy.

She had to turn off her feelings…deny the single most significant emotion that had led her into the field of nursing.

There could be no compassion in this equation.

She would feel nothing—except determination to do the unthinkable…to lead Cole Danes to his execution.

Chapter Four

The residence of Angel Parker, Winnetka, 6:28 p.m.

Cole watched the house for some time from his rental car and the cover of the dark winter evening. Halfway up the block a street lamp struggled to illuminate the night but failed miserably. No one stirred. The evening rush hour had passed. Dinner and television would be on the agenda for most of the residents of this quiet neighborhood.

Inside the small home he monitored there were no lights, no sound. But her car sat in the driveway. He checked his thermal scanner once more. There was definitely a warm body inside.

He deposited the scanner back into his pocket and withdrew his cell phone. When he'd entered the necessary numbers, he waited as the telephone inside Angel Parker's house rang three times.

"Hello."

A moment passed before he depressed the end call button.

From that single word of greeting he'd concluded three significant factors. Angel was inside. She felt defeated. But she wasn't afraid.

The latter intrigued him.

She should be afraid.

He unsheathed his weapon and exited the vehicle, the interior lamps set to the off position to ensure no interruption in his cloak of darkness. He wore black, always did, as much for intimidation as for camouflage. In any interrogation setting the tone proved every bit as crucial as the interrogator's skill.

No textbook or classroom exercise offered by the traditional means had taught him those essential elements. He had learned the unvarnished truth about interrogation the hard way, as a prisoner and hostage. His work had allowed him to hone his methods. Wisdom earned from a decade of experience in the field had boiled all he'd gleaned down to one basic fact, fear proved a far more advantageous weapon than pain.

He needed Angel Parker to feel fear.

Before this night ended she would know its true meaning. That fear would ultimately save her.

Cole paused outside the front entrance to the quiet house. He considered the owner for a moment, then the layout of the property. Small, well-groomed front yard with a postage-stamp-size lawn. Neat sidewalk lined with clay pots he imagined would be filled to brimming with flowers in the spring and summer. A tiny stoop, a welcoming wreath on the front door. The backyard looked much the same with a bit more grass and a child's swing set.

He estimated that his target sat approximately five yards from the front door. He listened intently for ten seconds. Still no sound. That she hadn't moved since his arrival forty-five minutes ago warned that she waited for something or someone.

His steps silent, he moved around to the back of the house. He curled his fingers around the knob of the rear entry and discovered the door unlocked. A red flag went up. The defeat he'd heard in her voice nudged at him. She thought she'd lost this battle already. Her child had been unaccounted for during the past three days. That would certainly defeat any caring parent.

The door opened noiselessly. Cole entered in the same way, every step carefully calculated for optimum stealth. He moved slowly through a tiny kitchen and into a short hall, giving his eyes time to adjust to the lack of moon and starlight he'd used outside. A subtle fragrance lingered in the air, apples and cinnamon. Some sort of potpourri, he surmised. The interior temperature felt too cool as if she hadn't bothered to turn on the heat on this cold winter day.

He waited at the doorway leading into the living room until he'd determined her exact location and gauged her posture using the sparse moonlight that filtered in through the window.

Cole leveled his weapon and moved toward her. She sat on a sofa, very dark in color, navy or forest-green perhaps. She wore dark slacks but the light color of her sweater or blouse kept her from totally disappearing into the opaque furniture. And there was her hair. Very blond, white almost. It fit with her name. She had the pale complexion and translucent blue eyes often associated with heavenly creatures. But this woman was not only very much from this earth, she definitely was not innocent. He paused in front of the coffee table, less than six feet from her position.

"Turn on the light."

She gasped at the sound of his voice.

As long as she'd been sitting there in the dark her reaction surprised him somewhat. Her eyes had surely adjusted to the near darkness. She should have noticed his presence when he'd entered the room, should have felt the shift in the atmosphere around her. But she hadn't. Clearly she'd been preoccupied with her thoughts.

"Please just tell me that my aunt's okay," she pleaded, assuming he was one of the men involved with Howard Stephens, Errol Leberman's murdering partner.

"Slowly reach for the lamp on the table next to you," he instructed firmly, ignoring her plea.

She obeyed, using her left hand. She was right-handed. His grip tightened on his weapon.

A *click* sounded and light spilled from the lamp.

The gun in her hand registered in that same instant, visually confirming his suspicion.

"Who the hell are you?" she demanded.

Maybe she hadn't lost all hope. She stared up at him with pure hatred, both hands now firmly locked around the 9mm. She'd purchased herself some protection recently. Illegally no doubt. There was no weapon registered in either her name or her aunt's.

"Lower your weapon," he countered, "and we'll talk."

She made a scoffing sound. "You lower yours," she tossed right back. "I'm not stupid."

No. She wasn't stupid. Just not wise in the ways of kill or be killed. He could have squeezed off a round and ended her life several times since the conversation began, while she still contemplated what would happen next.

"If I wanted you dead, Miss Parker, you would already be dead." He nodded to the table that stood between them. "Put it there. Use your left hand."

She blinked, long lashes momentarily hiding the fear in those pale eyes. "No."

"Then you leave me no choice."

Before she could comprehend his intent he had snaked out his left hand, snagged the weapon and twisted it out of her grasp. She rocketed to her feet but froze when the barrel of his weapon leveled back on her chest.

"Sit."

"What else do you want from me?" she demanded. She started to shake. Panic…adrenaline. She was on the edge, but not quite where he needed her.

"I think you have me confused with some of your longtime associates."

Her expression turned bewildered but only for a moment, realization dawned. "You're…" She moistened her lips as if buying time to marshal the additional effort required to utter his name. "You're Cole Danes."

"Sit down, Miss Parker."

She eased down onto the navy slipcovered sofa. From what he knew of her finances the old sofa had likely been covered out of necessity rather than design.

"Three days ago your daughter disappeared, then twenty-four hours later your aunt vanished. I know you were involved with Howard Stephens as far back as two years ago. I also know that the disappearances of the people you care about are connected to him and certain information involving the Colby Agency." The first glitter of true terror appeared in her eyes. "I already know the worst of what you've done, Miss Parker, so start talking and don't leave anything out."

Angel had no idea what Cole Danes looked like. But, whoever this man was, he had her gun. Fear knotted in her stomach. Why hadn't she just shot him?

Because she couldn't.

The men holding her aunt hostage wanted Cole Danes. If she killed him…God she didn't even want to think about what they would do to her aunt. What was she thinking? She couldn't kill anyone.

She clasped her hands in her lap in an effort to disguise their trembling and took a deep breath. The man on the phone had told her to follow Danes's lead.

Her gaze moved back up to the man standing over her. "If you know so much why do I have to tell you anything?" She didn't have to make this easy for him. He was her enemy just as much as the other two were. She couldn't trust anyone. Not even the people Mildred trusted at the Colby Agency. They had sent *this man* after her.

The Colby Agency couldn't help her. Not that she could blame Victoria for hating her now. The idea of what her actions had put the woman through…Angel shuddered.

The police couldn't help her, either.

She was on her own.

"Don't try my patience, Miss Parker."

What she saw in his eyes more than the sound of his voice warned her that he was not a man who liked games. The intensity in those blue eyes unnerved her completely. It didn't help that he had long hair secured in a ponytail and a silver hoop in one earlobe. She shivered. He looked as if he belonged on a seventeenth-century pirate ship rather than in her living room. But she'd seen guys like him in contemporary movies. Always ruthless, always ignoring laws other than their own.

"All right." She closed her eyes briefly and prayed that those other men wouldn't storm her house just now and kill them both before she could at least attempt to find her aunt. She had no way of knowing their intentions. She could only do as she was told.

She didn't know why she bothered, but she decided to tell Mr. Danes the truth to the extent she could. Why add one more transgression to her rising tally of sins to answer for? she reasoned. Right now, she considered morosely, going to hell was the least of her worries.

"Two years ago a man approached me at work and asked for scheduling information regarding Victoria Colby." She shrugged. "I thought it was some sort of joke until he told me that he had my daughter and that I wouldn't get her back until he had the information. I argued that I had no way of getting what he wanted and he countered that all I had to do was access the agency's system through my aunt's ID."

God it seemed so long ago now. She shook her head slowly from side to side. "I went to my aunt's office for lunch that same day and while she was in Victoria's office, I looked at her computer. Got what they asked for." She swallowed back a lump of remembered emotion. "They gave me my daughter back and threatened that if I ever told anyone that they would kill her next time."

"So you told no one," Danes prompted. "You didn't trust your aunt enough to tell her."

Angel glared at him. "Do you think I'd risk my child's life? I couldn't take the chance." She'd done the right thing. Like now, what other choice was there?

"Howard Stephens was the man who came to you for information from time to time?" he asked.

She nodded. "I didn't know his name for a long time. It was all done anonymously. Once in a while he or one of his men would be waiting at the child-care center where I took my daughter just to prove they could get to her. They even came in my house in the middle of the night. I'd find my baby's crib empty." Tears burned her eyes. "I'd search the house frantically only to find her sleeping in her playpen." She looked up at the man no doubt passing judgment on her at that very moment. "They would do this just to prove they could. To keep me aware of who held all the power."

"How did you manage to hide your daughter this time?"

A new kind of fear froze in her veins. "I won't tell you where she is. Even if you torture me, I won't say."

Apparently he believed her since he moved on.

"Something tipped you off, gave you the opportunity to get one step ahead."

"Aunt Mildred told me about Victoria Colby's son." Colby-Camp, she reminded herself. Victoria was now married to Lucas Camp. "When she explained all that this evil man Leberman had done I realized that his actions in the past two years coincided with information I had given Stephens." A heavy breath pushed past her lips. She would never forgive herself for what she'd had to do. She certainly didn't expect God or anyone else to. "I hoped that since Leberman was dead that it was over. I couldn't imagine any reason his men would continue to haunt my life or Victoria's."

She let go a weary breath. "But about a week ago Aunt Mildred told me about the investigation and that there might be a leak at the agency. I knew then it wasn't over."

"Get up."

His command startled her. "What?"

"Get up."

She pushed to her feet, uncertain whether he intended to kill her or…some part of her brain wondered if Stephens's men had anticipated this move. Did Victoria Colby-Camp want revenge for what Angel had done? Angel could scarcely blame her. But she hadn't known Victoria's missing child was related to those evil men…hadn't been able to do anything else.

"You have five minutes to pack whatever you think you need."

She blinked, confused all over again. So he wasn't going to kill her?

But where was he taking her? Would those men be watching? Was this part of their plan?

She shoved her hair behind her ears and reached for some semblance of composure. Didn't matter. She had her instructions.

She grabbed her purse from the floor and made her way to the bedroom. Cole Danes stayed right behind her, his weapon carefully trained on her back. She didn't have to look to know, she could feel it.

Somewhere she had an overnight bag. She prowled through the closet until she found it. A nightshirt, a couple of changes of undergarments, sweaters and jeans. Oh, yeah, and socks. Too cold to go without them. Toothbrush, toothpaste. Antiperspirant. She couldn't think of anything else.

"Get your coat and let's go."

She faced him, the weight of her bag dragging at her right shoulder. "Where are we going?" Surely he wouldn't turn her in to the police. Lord, she hadn't thought of that until that very second. What she had done was criminal. She could go to prison. Her aunt would die and her child would be raised by strangers. All of which, she admitted, a new flood of oppression washing over her, would likely happen anyway.

"No questions."

She resisted when he took her arm and would have ushered her from the room. The other man, the one who worked for Howard Stephens, had said those same words. *No questions.*

How could she be sure this was Cole Danes? What if she went with this man and it was a mistake?

"I need to see some ID." She tugged her arm free of his firm grasp, knowing she couldn't have done so had he not allowed it. He was strong. Tall, broad shouldered, but lean and powerful like a panther.

He reached into his jacket with his free hand and withdrew a leather case. "Be my guest."

She took the case from him and opened it. The picture on the credentials was this man all right. Six-two, one hundred seventy pounds. Forty. That surprised her. He didn't look more than thirty-five. Lived in Washington D.C. She handed the case back to him. She didn't want to know anything else.

"Convinced?"

"I suppose." Credentials could be forged. She didn't see the point in bringing that to his attention. He would likely know.

He slipped the case back into his interior pocket then motioned to the door with his gun. She reached for a jacket in her closet and tugged it on.

"Back door," he said when she would have turned toward the living room.

Angel drew in a long, deep breath of cool night air as Danes hustled her across her neighbor's backyard. The moon did little to light their path but he apparently knew where he wanted to go. He moved in the night like most people did in the daylight, without hesitation or conscious thought. Even she didn't know her neighbor's yard so well.

When they'd crossed to the opposite side of the street, he waited beneath the shadow of a copse of trees before resuming the journey to wherever he'd parked.

A dark sedan eased up to the curb in front of her house. Angel peered through the darkness and tried to see who got out. Two people. Tall. Male, she decided, after surveying their bulky frames.

Stephens's men.

One moved stealthily toward her front door while the other crossed the street and searched a car parked there.

More lights came on inside her house.

The guy at the car swore hotly then moved quickly to join his friend in her house.

"What—"

The rest of her query died in her throat as Danes's hand closed over her mouth. When she struggled his arm clamped around her waist and hauled her against him. His body felt hard against her backside. His arm a band of unyielding steel.

The two men suddenly burst out through her front door and rushed to the car they had arrived in. She couldn't make out their gruff dialogues before they'd piled into the vehicle and sped away.

The man who'd called had told her to follow Danes's lead. Was she supposed to have kept him at her house until they arrived? Had she somehow made a mistake?

Fear exploded inside her. Would they kill her aunt now? Start the search for her child? No. No! Please, God. No.

Danes released her. Her knees gave way beneath her.

All that kept her from an up-close encounter with the ground was his swift reaction. He had her back in his powerful arms in the nick of time. Her mind whirled with more questions…mounting fear. What did she do now?

"Can you walk?" He shook her when she didn't respond. "I said, can you walk?"

She nodded and grappled to regain her equilibrium. "Yes."

He took her bag, draped it over his own shoulder and then she was suddenly moving forward… through the dark, through more yards that weren't her own. His punishing grip on her wrist lugging her in his path.

"Where are we going?"

"Shut up."

He had to know something she didn't, knew those men would be out looking for them. "Are they searching for us now?"

He halted abruptly and his face was suddenly right

in front of hers. His grip had somehow relocated from her wrist to her chin. "If you want to live, *shut up*."

She trembled. Bit down on her lower lip to hold back a pained yelp. His fingers tightened. "No more talking."

He started forward again, his viselike grip on her wrist once more. She thought about the gun she'd bought. The advice the man at the pawnshop had given her. Why hadn't she shot him when he told her to turn on the light? Why had she let him take her gun away?

Those men wanted him. They were angry that they'd missed him. Somehow she had made a mistake, was supposed to have kept him occupied until they arrived.

Wait.

Her frantic thoughts jarred to a stop.

They wanted to teach Danes a lesson first. He'd said that. She remembered now. Maybe this was part of the lesson—a sick game of some sort. But how was that possible? It felt wrong. As if Danes was in control. She'd heard the man who'd checked the car swear. He'd been furious. If things had gone as he'd planned why would he be angry?

Danes suddenly stopped.

He opened the passenger-side door of a black SUV. Did it belong to him? If so, why had the other man thought the car parked across the street from her house belonged to Danes? Had he thought that at all? She couldn't be sure. She'd assumed. None of this made sense now.

"Get in."

"Is this your car?" She shook her head. "What about the car parked across the street from my house?"

"Pay attention," he growled as he pulled her intimidatingly near. "Get in."

He'd told her to shut up. Her skin still burned where he'd held her chin. She nodded and climbed into the seat. He leaned in over her. She sank as far into the leather seat as possible, but it wasn't enough. His scent, something too subtle to distinguish, invaded her senses. The hard feel of his shoulder as she braced her hand against it in an effort to push him away, but he was far too strong. He withdrew something from his pocket and moved it over her purse. Small, black. A red light flashed on the small object.

He opened her purse and rifled through the contents,

"What're you doing?" she demanded when he pulled out the lipstick she carried. She didn't know why she bothered carrying it, she never used it.

He tossed the lipstick then moved his hand down the length of her legs, over her torso. Even in the sparse moonlight the intensity in his eyes unsettled her all the more. He checked her overnight bag in the same manner.

When he was satisfied he closed her door, swiftly skirted the hood, tossed her bag into the back seat and slid behind the steering wheel.

He'd driven to the end of the block and turned onto the main thoroughfare before he switched on the headlights. Angel tugged her seat belt into place and bit back the questions that rushed into her throat. She'd watched movies where devices were used to track the movement of vehicles and people. Is that why that red light had flashed on her purse and then he'd tossed her lipstick? She didn't dare ask.

This couldn't be happening. She rubbed at her eyes. Tried to think. Her hands shook so badly. She clasped them together and reached for a calm she knew she would not find.

Pay attention.

He'd told her to pay attention. That's what she needed to do. Where were they going? He took one turn after the other. Taking his time, moving forward a few blocks and then to the left. A right, then forward through a couple of intersections. He made it difficult to follow but she finally decided that the interstate was his destination though she couldn't be absolutely certain until he'd taken the turn.

I-94 South.

Chicago.

Fear crashed into her. Was he taking her to the Colby Agency? Maybe he did intend to turn her over to the authorities.

To her surprise, once on the interstate, he took the first exit that came into view. Her heart pounded hard against her sternum. Where was he going now? She tried to think what was on this exit. He wheeled into the parking lot of a small motel and drove all the way to the back of the parking lot. Her fear mounted.

He got out, reached in the back seat for her bag then flashed her a look that told her in no uncertain terms to get out. At the front of the vehicle he latched on to her arm again and led her to a lower-level room. When he jammed the keycard into the lock she couldn't keep quiet any longer.

"What are we doing here?"

He ushered her inside and locked the door.

After a survey of the room with the same device he'd used on her purse he dropped her bag on the floor and shouldered out of his jacket. He tossed it onto the foot of the bed as if he intended to stay awhile.

"Enough." She'd had it. "What the hell are you doing? Why did you bring me here?"

He simply stared at her.

She hugged her arms around her middle. "They're going to kill my aunt," she said, her voice lacking enough strength to actually call her words a success-ful plea. It was too late…she knew it. She'd screwed up somehow.

He moved closer, that intense gaze searching her

face. Maybe he would feel sorry for her and help her. She didn't care if he saved her…if he would only help her aunt, protect her child.

"Please," she murmured, desperation urging her to act. "You have to help her."

He moved so suddenly, so lightning fast that he'd pinned her against the wall before she'd realized he'd moved at all. The air rushed out of her lungs more from the intensity of his eyes than the impact. "Don't presume that we're on the same side," he whispered fiercely, his face so close to hers she could feel his breath on her lips.

A new kind of fear synapsed in her brain, igniting every cell in its path with sheer terror.

"When I told you to talk, I wanted everything. Clearly, you left out a few details."

He knew.

How could he know?

Oh, dear God. He'd tapped her phone. He had to have heard the conversation…but then why ask?

"I know they contacted you earlier this evening."

Was it her imagination or had the pressure of his touch eased slightly? The fear throbbing inside her made it difficult to judge.

"Yes," she relented. She had to breathe, once, twice. "One of them called."

His hold relaxed. "What were his instructions?"

He didn't know. Relief trickled into the mix of churning emotions. He might have been listening but somehow he hadn't been able to hear…to understand… Something.

She still had a chance here. This had to be part of whatever they'd planned for Danes. *Some kind of crazy game.* But why would they want to play games? So much didn't make sense. He'd said he wanted to teach Danes a lesson. For what?

Danes waited for her to answer. He hadn't drawn his weapon yet but she knew he would if she didn't tell him more. She had to be careful. She couldn't reveal too much.

"They…" She tried to slow her respiration. The quick, shallow breaths would only make her hyperventilate. "They told me to wait for you. That you would be coming." She looked into those analyzing eyes and prayed he wouldn't see the lie in hers. "That's what I did. That's why I went out and bought a gun today." She relaxed a fraction when his expression didn't change. "I didn't know what would happen."

His stare…the silence…went on for so long that she felt a line of sweat bead on her forehead. *Please, please, let him believe me.* She knew it was wrong to pray for that kind of deception, but she was desperate. God knew just how desperate.

He drew slightly back, his gaze never leaving hers. "You're lying."

Her pulse jumped as his hold grew brutal once more. "No… No. I'm not lying." She shook her head adamantly. "All they want is you." Was that too much? She had to say something more. He'd seen through her deception. "You're all they want," she insisted. "If I stayed put and let you come after me they would release my aunt unharmed."

There was something about the way he looked at her then that sent a chill straight to the marrow of her bones.

"How valiant of you." The words were barely more than a whisper but even then she heard in his silky voice just how much he despised her.

She closed her eyes and fought back the humiliating tears. He was right to feel that way. All of this was because of her. Her child was living with strangers, her aunt being held hostage, this man's life on the line because of what she'd done.

Because of her mistake.

"I'm sorry." She moistened her lips and tried to take a breath but her chest felt too tight. "This isn't about you. This is my fault." She looked directly into those accusing eyes. "He told me my aunt would be safe if I did exactly as he said."

"The chances that your aunt is still alive are slim to none," he said bluntly. Her heart wrenched at the cold words. "If you're leaving anything out to protect her, don't waste my time. Think about your daughter, Miss Parker. These are not the kind of men who leave loose ends. Your aunt is likely already dead. They will kill you, that's a given. Then they'll kill your little girl just for the sport of it. It's what they do."

Despite her best efforts hot tears streamed down her cheeks. "Then what am I supposed to do?" How could she trust this man? If she told him the rest…she couldn't do that.

"I'm the only chance you've got of surviving. You can either trust me or we'll both end up dead."

He backed off physically but that penetrating stare never deviated. "Get some sleep. Think about what I said. Let me know what you decide."

Sleep. She frowned.

Her gaze flew to the digital clock on the bedside table.

7:56 p.m.

Panic broadsided her. "But we don't have time."

He moved in close again, his size, his scent, the way he studied her, terrified her all over again. "What's the hurry, Miss Parker? We're safe for the moment."

"He said I had forty-eight hours," she confessed, defeated. She couldn't do this anymore. "Forty-eight hours or she would die."

"Forty-eight hours for what?"

Every debilitating emotion she'd felt…every horrible moment she'd lived through these past few days crowded in on her at once. Her mistakes. Those awful men taking her aunt away. The call. The waiting.

Cole Danes.

The sudden, foolish desire to trust him…to believe in anything even remotely right in this insane situation.

"To make sure you walked into their trap." There. She'd said it. "To teach you a lesson," she explained. "They plan to play some sort of game with you first. Someone will contact me with the next step. That's all I know."

For the space of three excruciating heartbeats he didn't react…just kept up that relentless stare.

"Very good, Miss Parker." A grim smile lifted the corners of his hard mouth. "Now we're on the same side."

Chapter Five

9:15 p.m.
37 hours remaining...

"Why do they want you?"

Perched on the edge of the mattress, Angel Parker had considered him at length before asking her question. Cole felt reasonably certain that she'd spent that time working up the courage to do so.

He wondered if a woman so young, barely twenty-five, and inexperienced in the ways of his world could even begin to comprehend the actual answer to that question.

Cole dismissed the possibility without further deliberation. He'd achieved his goal, prodded her fear factor until she reached a vulnerable zone in order for him to obtain the required information. She knew nothing else of value at this time. Her continued participation in this matter was merely a technicality to ensure the link between him and his target.

"Do..." She dropped her gaze to her hands

briefly before meeting his once more. "Do you know these men?"

"Do you?" He increased the intensity of his stare several degrees. She looked away again. Didn't like the way he analyzed her. Not a particularly burdensome task from his vantage. Angel Parker was quite attractive. Slender, maybe too much so, medium height. Her white blond hair and clear blue eyes made him think of faraway places. But her lips were her most distracting asset by far. Overly full, incredibly lush. The kind of lips women with the means sought from skilled surgeons.

She licked those lush lips genetics had provided, the movement sparked by discomfort at his presence. Angel Parker was not an overtly sexual creature. Not that he doubted her ability to be infinitely sexual, she simply concealed her appeal. Or perhaps she was not aware of that power. No, he amended. That conclusion gave her more credit than he was prepared to give at this time. She was no innocent.

"I know Howard Stephens," she said in answer to his question. "But I don't know this new man…the one who gave me the instructions this time. I'd never met him before." She stared at her hands once more. "Mr. Stephens is the one who wanted to know your name. He took my aunt."

"Howard Stephens is dead."

Slowly, as if afraid of what she might see, she

lifted her gaze to his. "Did you kill him? Is that why these men are after you now?"

He watched her eyes grow wider, saw the fear tighten its noose.

"In a manner of speaking," he allowed, uncertain why he bothered to tell her anything. He had set things in motion. His intricate planning had ensured the outcome.

"I don't understand." She sucked in an unsteady breath. "Why are they doing this to me? They got what they wanted from my aunt." She searched his face. "Why don't they let her go? Why are they using us to get to you? My aunt had no part in any of this."

Cole leaned forward and braced his forearms on his widespread knees. "Because they can."

"So you do know who these men are?"

"Yes."

She dropped her hands to the mattress on either side of her. Her fingers curled in the covers as if she needed to hang on. "What do we do now? We can't just keep waiting. Time is running out." Her voice grew more frantic with each word. Pumping up her fear had been necessary, but he didn't need her hysterical.

"He'll call."

"How can you be sure?" She trembled but quickly staunched the telling reaction. "We've been sitting here for over an hour. They might not call. Maybe I did something wrong. Maybe they know you're on to their plan."

"He will call. I'm well aware of how these men operate. Waiting is our only option."

She lunged to her feet and started to pace the small room. He monitored her escalating apprehension but made no move to interfere. Let her walk off the adrenaline. Fatigue would do its work in time.

"I bought that weapon to protect myself." She whirled to face him, anger fueling, renewing her determination. "I convinced myself I could kill that man if I had to." A visible shudder went through her, testing her hold on composure. "Told myself I could kill you if that's what it took." She scrubbed at her forehead with a shaky hand. "But I couldn't. I couldn't do it." Her watery gaze found his once more. "And now my aunt is going to die because I'm too weak to help her."

She rushed to where he sat and dropped to her knees. "I have a three-year-old daughter. She needs me. Isn't there something you can do to help us? I have to get through this for my daughter," she urged, then her face fell. "But I don't think I'll be able to live with myself if my aunt dies because of my mistake."

She had no idea how dangerous this game really was. Not a clue. As guilty as she was for succumbing to Stephens's ploy in the first place, there was no denying the lack of malice and calculation in her personality, though he wanted to do just that. Her only crime, he realized, was a lack of intelligent reasoning and foresight triggered by extreme fear.

She lifted her gaze to his, only inches separating them. "Please help me. Don't you have any children of your own? A wife? Family somewhere? You must know how this feels. How it could end."

She was right about one thing, he already knew how this would likely end. "Don't waste your time attempting to play on my sympathies," he warned, purposely adding an air of danger to his tone. "I've never felt the need for a wife or children. And empathy is not one of my strong points."

She sat back on her heels and studied him, surprisingly not put off by his strategy. Her gaze moved over his every feature, his eyes, across his forehead, along the bridge of his nose, and the line of his jaw, then to his mouth. A frown disturbed her smooth forehead as she assessed his hard features. The sudden, almost irresistible urge to touch that troubled skin caught him off guard. He refrained from touching her but refused to draw away, instead he remained perfectly still, allowed her to look at her leisure. She would only see what he wanted her to see. Nothing more.

"You think you don't need anyone, don't you?" Those translucent eyes met his with a kind of knowing that sent a chord of uneasiness through him. "You think you've got everything figured out and that you're above it all. You're wrong."

He seized her wrist and held her close when she would have moved away. "I'm never wrong, Miss Parker."

Any lingering fear had vanished from her eyes. There was only a certainty that infuriated him.

"This time you are."

Angel wasn't sure how she'd worked up the nerve to argue with him on that particular point but the realization that she'd broken through some barrier was palpable. She'd gotten to him somehow. The burst of fury that darkened his eyes made her shiver. She should be afraid. Every instinct warned her that she should be seriously afraid and, yet, she wasn't. She felt calmer than she had in days.

He smiled then, widely, an intimate awareness in his eyes that stole her calm as abruptly as if he'd jerked a rug out from under her feet.

"Need is a very misunderstood element of the human psyche, Miss Parker." His voice was like silk, smooth, rich, but there was no mistaking an underlying lethal quality. "One either attends to it or denies it. When I experience a need, I satisfy it and walk away." His fingers tightened around her wrist. "What I need right now is for you to do exactly as I say and nothing more. Do you understand?"

She nodded, the movement uncoordinated.

"Get some rest." He released her. "There's nothing more we can do until he calls."

Angel pushed to her feet and backed away from him. She bumped into the mattress and let gravity drag her down to it. She closed her eyes to block him from her sight. There would be no reaching this man.

She'd been stupid to try. He was as ruthless as the men holding her aunt hostage.

A medley of musical notes cracked the thick tension, yanking her from her disturbing thoughts. *Her cell phone.* She scrambled across the bed and grabbed her purse.

Danes manacled her wrist before she could depress the button to accept the call. "Be very careful what you say. Let him hear your fear. Show your eagerness to do whatever he asks."

His words elicited a powerful bolt of both emotions. "What if he asks about you?" What was she supposed to say then? The second cluster of notes pealed. Anticipation urged her to answer the call.

"Tell him the truth, that I'm holding you hostage."

She blinked. Was she a hostage? The idea startled her though it shouldn't have.

"Answer the call *now.*"

Her pulse jumped at the savage sound of his voice. *Wait. Hurry. We're on the same side now.* All of it was too confusing.

Stay calm. Think rationally.

She depressed the necessary button and held her breath. "Hello." She refused to consider how fragile she sounded. Blocked out the image of Cole Danes towering over her.

"Is he with you?"

Him. The man. She recognized him instantly. "Yes."

"Good."

His response caused a hitch in the breath she finally released.

"What am I supposed to do?" Sound eager. Was that eager enough? God, she didn't know.

"Is he listening?"

She nodded then caught herself. "Yes. He's right here."

The sinister rasp of a ruthless chuckle vibrated across the line. "Excellent. Tell him to take you to Lincoln Park at dawn. I'll be waiting."

"What about my aunt?" *Please, please, let my aunt be safe,* she prayed.

"I'll release her as soon as Cole Danes is dead."

Angel squeezed her eyes shut and pressed the heel of her hand against her forehead. She wanted to cry…wanted to demand that this bastard let her aunt go. None of this was Mildred's fault. *She* had caused all of this. She was the guilty one.

"Take me," she murmured. "You can have me instead. Please. Just let her go. And stay away from my daughter."

"Oh, but I need you right where you are, *Angel,*" he cajoled hatefully. "You see, I want Cole Danes dead and you're going to help me make that happen."

She started to shake with something besides fear and anticipation. Rage blazed through her. "There's nothing I can do! Don't you see that?"

"The only thing I need to see is you *and Danes* at dawn."

He disconnected.

She wanted to scream.

Danes took the phone from her hand and turned it off.

"What're you doing?" She vaulted off the bed to put herself on more even ground with him. "He might try to call back." Was he out of his mind? She needed that connection!

"He won't. He's given you your instructions."

"Leave it on just in case." Why risk it? She reached for her phone but he held it away.

"That call established a link," he told her. "If we leave on the phone he can track our location."

Defeat sagged at her shoulders. "Why would he do that? He wants us to meet him at Lincoln Park at dawn. Why bother setting up a location if he planned to come after us now?"

"Insurance," he insisted calmly, too damn calmly. "He would prefer to track our movements. That's why we're going to stay one step ahead of him."

She sliced her arms through the air, sick of his persistent calm. "This is crazy. The two of you are playing games and my aunt is in danger." An epiphany flashed in her brain, the possibility so disarming she trembled at the idea. "Do you know more than you're telling me?"

"Give me the rest of what he said and then get some sleep otherwise you'll be useless come dawn."

She grabbed his arm in an attempt to make him

understand that she needed to know. The hard muscle beneath her fingers brutally drove home the point she did not want to face. How was she supposed to contend with this kind of strength and determination? But she had to try.

"What is it you're not telling me? You know something." She was operating in the dark here. Didn't he know that? If he had more information, he needed to share it with her. Surely he wouldn't stand back and risk her aunt's life…surely he didn't know the worst already…. Had he said something to that effect?

"What else did he say to you?"

She let go of him and pressed her fingertips to her temples. She felt confused…afraid. She didn't know what to do. The gun had been her only means of fighting back. She had nothing. She looked straight at Cole Danes. Only this man. A man void of emotion. Defeat settled heavily onto her shoulders.

"Start at the beginning."

Well, he was her only chance. She had no choice but to work with him.

"He wanted to know if you were here," she told him wearily. "I said yes. Then he wanted to know if you were listening. I said yes again. He wants you to take me to Lincoln Park at dawn."

"What did he tell you about Mildred Parker? What was his response to your offer of trading yourself for your aunt?"

She glared up at him. "He wouldn't tell me anything. Said he needed me here, that I was going to help him kill you and that my aunt wouldn't be released until you were dead." She flung the words at him like missiles intended to wound, but his emotions were impenetrable.

Danes inclined his head. "Interesting."

His reaction made her more certain than ever. "There's something more going on here. What is it you're not telling me?"

A new kind of tension thickened between them, the silence wholly unnerving, his unwavering gaze adding yet another layer of relentless strain.

"I know these men," he confessed though clearly he didn't want to tell her anything. "They're the final two members of the death squad Errol Leberman and Howard Stephens created. Both will die before this is over. *If* you get in my way, you'll die, too."

5:15 a.m.
29 hours remaining

COLE WATCHED the woman sleep. She'd tossed and turned for most of the night, but she'd finally surrendered to her body's need to shut down at 2:00 a.m.

He'd taken a few minutes of rest here and there, never indulging in more than that at any one time.

Dawn would arrive within the hour. It was time to wake her. Yet he hesitated. Preferred not to bother

her, she slept so peacefully now. Even in the uncharitable glow of the cheap bedside lamp, she looked agonizingly young. And innocent, he admitted. Leberman and Stephens had used her. She'd been afraid and had acted accordingly.

But her innocence or guilt were of no consequence. His mission could not be accomplished without her and for that reason it was necessary to keep her unbalanced, fearful. She was determined, he had to give her that. Her aunt's safety, as well as that of her child, appeared to be primary. Another unforeseen turn. He'd expected the child to hold precedence but not the aunt. Whether Angel fully realized it or not, her aunt's survival of this ordeal was not likely. Yet she would not give up on finding her unharmed. He had not anticipated that level of selflessness in one so young and seemingly focused on her own life.

Cole dismissed the surge of respect he experienced on the heels of those deductions. However selfless Angel Parker might be, she had brought this war down on herself. He had to bear that in mind. She was not completely innocent.

He refused to acknowledge the other nagging instinct. Something he hadn't felt for a very long time—ten years actually. A foolish part of him wanted to protect her from further damage. He stood, shook it off.

Hadn't he learned long ago that those with whom he dealt rarely deserved such a costly commodity?

The urge to protect, like compassion, served only one purpose: to make you weak. To steal crucial attention and energy.

He never made mistakes. He would not make one now.

Time to go. No more dwelling on a subject best left alone.

He moved to the bed where she lay and shook her, none too gently. "Wake up. It's time to go."

She sat up instantly, her heavy, long-lashed lids fluttering open. Her breath caught when memory identified him and reminded her of time and place.

She climbed out of bed without responding. Her hair was tousled, her clothes rumpled, but she didn't appear to care. She went directly to the bathroom and closed the door. Two minutes later she exited, her hair finger combed and her clothes straightened somewhat.

"I'm ready."

One look in her eyes told the truth of the matter. She wasn't ready, but she would do what she had to in an effort to help her aunt. To rid their lives of this curse once and for all.

He sent a pointed look at her bare feet.

"Oh." Her cheeks flushed. "I forgot." She quickly tugged on her sneakers without bothering to untie them.

"The jacket, too." He indicated the jacket lying on the end of the bed.

Angel shouldered into her well-worn denim jacket and let go a grave breath. Now or never.

"Get your purse," Danes said. "We won't be coming back here." He picked up her overnight bag and slung it over one broad shoulder.

She nodded and snagged her purse. "Can I turn on my cell phone now?"

"No."

She muttered an unflattering adjective under her breath.

He walked out the door ahead of her, surveyed the parking lot then motioned for her to follow. For a man who seemed to care about no one she couldn't help wondering why he bothered. Maybe he wasn't quite so ruthless as he wanted her to believe.

Streaks of gold-and-purple light had started to cut through the night, lending an ominous ambience to the cold, wet morning. She shivered as the frigid air penetrated her thin jacket.

Pull it together. Stay alert, she ordered. Wet from the rain that had fallen sometime during the night while she slept like the dead, the pavement looked inky black. A perfect morning for this sort of excursion, she supposed. Cold and ugly. Threatening.

Glass shattered next to her.

It took several seconds for Angel to realize the car window on her right, less than two feet back had burst as she passed it.

Suddenly she slammed downward...onto the

damp pavement. The impact knocked the air out of her lungs.

Danes was on top of her, firing his weapon rapidly, the sounds exploding in the air, deafening her.

"Get under the car."

She tried to comprehend his barked order but somehow she couldn't.

He shoved her toward the vehicle on her left. "Get under there now!"

She scooted on her belly. Didn't stop until she'd reached the middle. Her breath came in ragged spurts. The smell of oil and gasoline caused her to gag.

The loud thunder of Danes's gun echoed, the explosions followed by odd pings and more shattering glass. She saw a clip hit the ground near where he crouched. It looked much like the ones she'd purchased with her gun...only bigger.

Why was he shooting?

Her mind suddenly wrapped around the other strange sounds and the broken glass.

Silencers. Whoever was shooting at them had sound suppressors on their weapons.

Who would be shooting at them?

One step ahead. Danes had said they were one step ahead. He didn't want them to know this location. He'd been wrong. Who else could this be? They had to know. It had to be *them.*

Tires squealed.

Three, four, five more shots from Danes's weapon.

Silence.

She forced her thoughts to slow. Tried to gulp in a deep breath to steady her respiration.

Silence.

She could see Danes's leather shoes where he still crouched. She squeezed her eyes shut for a moment just to be sure the shadow of the image wasn't some-how burned on her retinas.

She looked again.

He was gone.

She jolted into action, sliding quickly from under the car. Sirens wailed in the distance. Faces peered from between the narrow gaps in drapes. No one moved between the parked vehicles. Broken glass. A car alarm throbbing.

Where was Danes?

She saw the man on the ground and was moving in that direction before the identity of the other man bent over him registered.

"Don't you die on me just yet, you son of a bitch," Danes snarled. He'd torn the man's shirt open. Blood seeped between his fingers where he attempted to staunch the flow from midtorso.

"We need an ambulance," Angel shouted back at the faces in the windows. Her purse…cell phone. The sirens. Someone had already called. She dropped to her knees on the other side of the man and checked his respiration and heart rate. Still breathing. Pulse thready. *Damn*.

"Tell me what I want to know," Danes growled.

The man tried to talk, his words too choked to understand.

"Don't try to talk," Angel told him before shooting Danes a glare. She surveyed the man again. "The ambulance is here," she told the man on the ground. "Hang on." Thank God someone had asked for an ambulance as well as the police. She could only assume that the call was made as soon as shots were fired for this kind of rapid response. The man's pulse rate was dropping.

Angel tried to assess the damage based on what she saw. She only knew that it was critical. Massive hemorrhaging. She couldn't do any more than Danes was already doing for that. Had the bullet exited? Turning him over was too risky.

Suddenly an EMT appeared next to her. She stood and immediately stepped back. This was EMT territory. They had the equipment. The second EMT moved into place next to Danes and initiated the IV while the other assessed the now unconscious patient's condition. She tried not to think about the fact that this man, though not the one who had shown up at her house yesterday, was likely involved in her aunt's kidnapping.

"I need this man alive," Danes said sharply.

The EMTs ignored the comment, conversed

quickly about the man's worsening condition, but Angel didn't really absorb their words; she couldn't get past what Danes had said. This couldn't be good. Where was the other man? Why had they shown up here? In her peripheral vision she caught a glimpse of two or three police officers headed their way.

"We have to get him to the hospital," the EMT said. "He needs surgery. *Now.*" The last he directed at Danes.

"Ma'am, can you tell me what happened here?"

The officer's voice tugged her attention from the scene on the ground. "I'm really not sure," she said hesitantly. "We came out of our room and this man—" she gestured to the ground but the EMTs had already loaded the patient onto a gurney and had headed to the waiting ambulance "—he…he started shooting at us." Sometime during the hail of bullets sunrise had lightened the sky. It seemed impossible that only moments ago she'd been hiding in the dark beneath that car.

The officer asked something else but Danes's climbing into the ambulance behind the two EMTs distracted her. "I'll be happy to answer your questions," she assured the officer. "Just let me check on…" She gestured to the ambulance.

"Of course, ma'am." Apparently he assumed she meant Danes. "But I'll need a statement from both you and your husband."

Maybe in some remote part of her brain she did

need to check on Danes. Had he been injured? She smiled faintly as the officer let her pass. She hurried toward the ambulance.

He thought she and Danes were a couple. The idea almost made her laugh. If her heart hadn't been beating so fast and her stomach hadn't been twisted around her esophagus she might have done just that.

She slowed at the rear doors of the vehicle, stunned somewhat that they hadn't rushed away before now. Was the man dead already? Was Danes hurt?

"Here are my credentials." Using one bloody hand Danes thrust the leather case he'd shown her last night in the man's face. He turned to the other EMT. "Now wake him up."

"Look man," the EMT with the credentials said. "I don't know anything about—"

"Who the hell is this guy?" the other one demanded of his partner, clearly not happy with Danes's orders.

His partner shrugged. "NSA."

"You know as well as I do that this man will not make it to the hospital," Danes said quietly, the intensity in the softer tone wholly unnerving. "He's dying. Now wake him up so I can question him."

The first EMT shoved the credentials case at Danes and looked at his partner. "We could try to bring him around with some epinephrine."

"Are you crazy?" his partner demanded. "We gotta roll with this guy."

Danes braced his hands on his hips, pushing the lapels of his jacket out of the way just far enough to display his shoulder holster and gun. "I don't care what you have to do. But do it here and now. *Wake him up.*"

Angel wanted to back away, didn't want to see this, but morbid fascination paralyzed her. She couldn't move…she could only watch as the eppie was administered, giving the man's heart rate and blood pressure a jolt to draw him back to consciousness.

Whatever his sins he was about to pay the ultimate price.

Her gaze settled on Danes.

She'd been wrong.

Cole Danes was far more ruthless than she'd even suspected.

Chapter Six

"Why are we coming back here?" Angel demanded as Danes ushered her back into the hotel room. "I thought you said—"

He secured the door then surveyed the parking area before pulling the drapes together more tightly. "We'll be safe here as long as those squad cars remain in the lot."

The blood on his hands, on hers, had dried, but the smell still haunted her. She'd never get used to that. Never. Her stomach roiled and she closed her eyes against the images and sounds. The gunfire...the blood. That man had died. What did that mean? A part of her couldn't help regretting the loss of human life, criminal or not.

"Take off your clothes."

She jerked to attention. Blinked twice. "What?"

"Take off all your clothes. Now."

He stared at her with that usual intensity, his

words perfectly clear, uttered in that brisk, cold tone, but she still didn't understand.

"Why do you want me to take off my clothes?" The idea seemed ludicrous given the current situation.

"Do it."

He strode into the bathroom and turned on the basin faucet. Dumbfounded, Angel watched as he scrubbed the blood from his hands. The nurse in her mentally ticked off the numerous diseases both of them would need to worry about. She stared at her own hands. They'd had to at least attempt to give the man aid until the ambulance arrived. For the good it had done. There had been so much blood. He most likely would not have survived... *Wake him up now.* She shuddered at the memory. Danes hadn't appeared to care if the man died, he'd wanted answers.

Had he gotten them? She'd turned away from the scene, hadn't been able to watch. The police officer had eventually wandered over and started his questioning again. Strangely, only minutes after the ambulance had left for the hospital with their patient who would be dead on arrival, the police had given them the go-ahead to leave, as well. Just another thing she didn't understand in any of this.

Who was Cole Danes that he could have a shootout in a public place, kill a man—in self-defense admittedly—and walk away with scarcely a comment to local law enforcement?

"I said take off your clothes."

She jumped at the sound of his voice. She had to get a hold of herself here. "Let me wash my hands." Another shudder rocked through her.

"In a moment."

He was serious. Dammit, she wasn't taking off her clothes without a good reason. "No." She shook her head adamantly. "Not until you tell me why."

"They knew to come here. We walked right into their trap. Maybe they locked in on our location during the call, but I don't think so. Tracking down a cell phone takes time. Either way, I'm not taking the chance that there's a bug I don't know about."

"But you checked me for bugs already." She remembered quite well the little thingie he'd used to scan her and her bags.

"New technology comes on the market every day. It's not impossible that he used something undetectable by the usual means."

She gestured to the bathroom. "I'll toss my clothes out to you."

He moved his head side to side. "It's not really your clothes I'm worried about. I need to inspect every square inch of your body."

Cole knew he'd shaken her with that request but it was necessary. "Now," he reiterated.

She hesitated a moment longer, likely grappling to find another excuse to argue the point with him. But, in the end, she was too smart not to see the obvious. Taking her slow, sweet time she shouldered out of her jacket and draped it on the foot of the bed.

He didn't like it when the target one-upped him and he'd definitely been one-upped this morning. But he had what he needed now. He would finish this, whatever the cost. The local police hadn't appreciated his refusal to cooperate. Nor had they been pleased at his ability to shift jurisdiction with a single phone call. And they definitely didn't like cleaning up someone else's mess. Cole didn't see the big deal. No civilians were harmed. Insurance would pay for any damage done to the vehicles in the lot. The only casualty was a man who'd overstayed his welcome on this planet years ago.

One left to go.

When that final piece of scum had ceased to share the same airspace as Cole he would at last be satisfied.

He'd waited ten long years to finish this.

She toed off her sneakers, rolled off the socks, then carefully placed the items next to her jacket.

In a show of his impatience, he folded his arms over his chest. The move sent pain slicing through his side. He gritted his teeth and ignored it. He'd endured much worse for far less. He would endure this. Time was short. The next move needed to be his.

The one remaining man was one he had studied well, knew almost as well as he knew himself. Not that finishing the matter would be simple, there were a number of complications, including Mildred Parker. But it would be an enjoyable task.

Angel's fingers moved to the buttons on her sweater. His gaze followed the release of each of three buttons at her throat. Stealing a quick glance in his direction, she crossed her arms in front of her and took hold of the hem of the sweater. The fabric slid up and over her head, landing on the bed with a good deal less care than the other items.

She looked directly into his eyes. "I'm not taking off my…" She cradled her arms in front of her breasts.

"I'll work around it," he allowed. Relief flooded her expression. "Stop stalling."

She turned her back and unfastened her jeans. The soft denim slid over her hips, revealing delicate bikini panties, the light pink color a perfect match to her bra. She lifted first one leg then the other to tug off the jeans. They plopped onto the bed. Timidly, her arms went up to shield as much of her torso as possible.

"What now?" she asked looking back over her shoulder at him.

Cole stood very still, his attention oddly distracted by her skin. It looked incredibly smooth, like porcelain. Her white-blond hair draped halfway to her narrow waist. The silky tresses looked even softer against the sleek shell of her skin.

The idea that touching her would be a mistake flitted through his mind but he dismissed it. This inspection was essential to his success. Not sexual…not pleasurable in any way.

He closed the distance between them in two long strides. Using both hands he scooped up her hair and fingered slowly through it, searching for any kind of device. Something organic likely, perhaps even a device that deteriorated in time, maintaining its shape and function only long enough to provide location.

Her hair felt every bit as silky as he'd anticipated. Then his fingers moved to her skin. She gasped. He recoiled abruptly at the warm feel beneath his fingertips. The smooth texture he'd anticipated, but not the warmth. Her flesh had looked too pale and sleek to be this warm. Bracing himself, he lowered his fingers there once more. Slid the tips over her shoulders, closely searched the flawless surface with his eyes as well as his touch.

"When they took your aunt away," he began, his voice strained somehow, "did either of the men touch you in any way? Brush against you?"

She shook her head, the movement sending long tendrils of pure silk swaying across her shoulders. "Not that I can recall. They…" She inhaled an unsteady breath. "They mostly just grabbed my arm."

Cole was surprised to see his hands shaking slightly as he moved toward the closure of her bra. He squeezed them into fists then relaxed. He clenched his jaw and focused. He had a job to do. He reached for the closure and unfastened it. She shivered, he did the same. The reaction annoyed him.

"Wait."

She turned slightly, staring up at him over her bare shoulder. The image tugged at something inside him which only made him angrier at himself.

"I almost forgot," she rushed to say. "They took our coats. I remember now that I forgot mine when they took me away afterward." A frown marred her smooth forehead. "Those two men, the one who died this morning and the other one who came to my house yesterday, drove my aunt and I to some place to question us. We were blindfolded so I don't know where."

"How long was the drive? Did you stay on paved streets?" Irrationally, Cole was thankful for the reprieve. At least he had time to regroup before touching her again.

"I…I'm not sure. I was so upset. Maybe thirty minutes."

Thirty minutes from her aunt's condo in Chicago. Angel had already told him that she'd gone to her aunt's place to tell her everything when the men arrived.

Angel pushed her hair back from her face and turned more fully toward him. "That man, the one who died this morning—" her gaze drifted to the window "—he searched us thoroughly. Made us open our blouses so he could see if we were wearing a wire or something like that."

Cole swore softly. "He knew you weren't wearing a wire," he snapped. "It was an excuse to get you to strip for him."

She looked mortified. "No…"

"Show me how he touched you," Cole ordered.

Angel tried to remember exactly what happened that night, but so much had happened…think! She had to think. She clutched her bra to her breasts with one arm and reached down to show him with the other.

"I remember he ran his hands over my sides." She focused hard on that horrifying moment. "All the way around to my spine. But he didn't have anything in his hand." She'd been so terrified, could she really say that with any real accuracy?

"Like this?" Danes flatted his palms against her abdomen, then slowly slid them around her waist.

Her breath trapped in her throat. Those wide, strong hands created a blaze wherever they touched. That intent blue gaze connected with hers and, knowing he wanted an answer, she nodded as best she could.

As he'd warned at the outset, he inspected every square inch of her torso from the sensitive area beneath her breasts to the rim of her panties. She couldn't look at him, though she knew he was looking at her. She could feel his eyes on her, watching, analyzing. She didn't want him to see the way his touch affected her. It was crazy. He was ruthless…uncaring…

"Don't move."

She opened her eyes in time to see him crouch down in front of her. He turned her slightly and inspected her left hip. She could feel his breath on her skin. Goose bumps skittered. Her fingers itched to touch his hair. To see if it felt as thick and silky as it looked. Despite the uncharacteristic length, the man had great hair. She closed her eyes and banished the crazy thought.

He lifted something from her skin and peered at it for a time before looking up at her. As startled as she was to see that he'd found something, for one moment she couldn't get past the vision of his face so close to her quivering belly.

"This is how they found us."

He stood and showed her the tiny transparent disk that had been stuck to her skin.

A line formed between her eyebrows as she stared at the near-invisible object. "I should have felt that?"

"You wouldn't. Certainly not under the circumstances."

He walked to the bathroom and flushed the disk down the toilet.

She looked at the dried blood on her hands and shuddered. "Can I wash up now?"

"You're certain he didn't touch you anywhere else?"

"I'm certain."

He nodded. "Clean up."

Angel couldn't say for sure right now since her own emotions were in a tailspin, but she got the distinct impression that Mr. Cold-As-Ice was uncomfortable.

Unbelievable.

10:00 a.m.
24 hours, 15 minutes remaining...

COLE WAITED in a parking garage downtown until the shops opened. He'd allowed Angel to take a shower, during which time he'd closely inspected the clothing she intended to wear. No more silent bugs. It annoyed him to no end that he hadn't considered that possibility. He should have.

"What're we doing?"

To her credit she hadn't asked any questions since they left the motel. He assumed that his seeing her undressed had unsettled her. Unfortunately it had rattled him to some degree. He didn't know what to make of that. Perhaps it was his proximity to finally achieving his goal that made him susceptible. Whatever the case, he was back on track now.

"We're going to make a few purchases and find a place to lie low until dark."

"Until dark?" Leather crinkled as she turned more fully toward him. "I only have twenty-four more hours. They're going to kill my aunt! I can't sit around waiting."

"He," Cole corrected.

She cut her hands through the air. "How the hell do you know there's only one guy left? He could have a dozen friends in on this with him."

"There's only one to be concerned with."

She plowed her fingers through her hair and heaved a sigh. "You can't be certain."

He leveled his gaze on hers. "I am certain."

"Whatever," she snapped. "We can't just sit here."

"What do you propose we do?" He injected a good measure of condescension in his tone to put her in her place. He doubted the strategy would be entirely successful but he had to try.

Her mouth dropped open but no words came out. From her frustrated expression he could see that she frantically searched for an option. One she wouldn't find.

"So we just wait for him to call again?"

"No." He removed the keys from the ignition. "We wait for nightfall."

He emerged from the SUV, which he had also swept thoroughly for alien electronic devices, and moved around to the passenger side.

He opened her door. "Get out."

"Didn't anyone ever teach you any manners, Mr. Danes?"

She climbed out to stand next to him. She waited, staring expectantly up at him. Apparently the question wasn't meant as a rhetorical one.

If he hadn't been so damn tired he might have been able to come up with a scathing reply that would shut her up but he lacked the energy to waste.

"Miss Parker, in case you've forgotten, I saved

your life this morning. Try and show a little gratitude."

"Not so fast." She snagged his arm when he turned away.

He produced the kind of stare that generally sent anyone of the species, male or female, into retreat. "What is it now?"

Her face turned grim. "What was it you asked the man you shot? What did he tell you?"

He'd expected her to get around to that eventually. She'd been too traumatized to inquire before now. Obviously, the shock had worn off to an extent.

"I asked him where they were keeping your aunt," he told her, seeing no point in hiding that fact from her.

She blinked, startled. "Did…did he tell you?"

"No."

A brutal blow of defeat punched Angel, making her sway. She was running out of time. In twenty-four hours her aunt would be dead. She wasn't any closer to finding her now than she had been when that bastard issued his ultimatum. What was she supposed to do?

The feel of Danes's hands on her arms, holding her steady, tugged her from the troubling thoughts.

"Sorry…I—" Why the hell was she apologizing to him? She pulled free of his hold. "Let's get this over with."

He escorted her to the major department store

next door to the parking garage. With an economy of time and effort he purchased a change of clothes for himself as well as for her. Apparently he wasn't taking any chances on more bugs.

Her suspicion was confirmed when he picked up another rental car at the airport, leaving his SUV in the short-term parking area. The only items she was allowed to keep were her purse and cell phone, which he had disassembled and reassembled in under a minute.

He pointed the new rental in the direction of town and drove for half an hour without saying anything.

"What are we doing now?" she asked as he finally parked midway along a crowded city block. She hated being left in the dark. He'd scarcely said a word since the exchange regarding the day's agenda in the parking garage nearly two hours ago.

He didn't bother responding, just got out and came around to her door. What was the point in arguing? He had the guns, hers included, he was in charge.

She followed him into the large corner drugstore, her mind drifting to her daughter. She tried not to think how long it had been since she'd seen her…held her. If she closed her eyes she could call to mind her daughter's sweet baby scent. Oh how she missed her. If she could just get through this and get back to her little girl…if her aunt was safe. She'd never ask God for anything else as long as she lived.

By the time her mind shifted back to the present, Danes had filled a small shopping basket with several items. She frowned as she attempted to identify the various goods. Gauze. Antibiotic ointment. Peroxide. A travel-size sewing kit. Gauze tape. A few male essentials, like a disposable razor and shaving cream. Two toothbrushes. Toothpaste.

Some of the items she could understand but what was with all the medical supplies?

Before she could question his selections he strode up to the counter and paid. Moments later they were in the car again. She didn't ask any questions because she sensed that he had no desire to talk. Instead, she studied his stony profile. As unyielding as the angular lines of his face, as hard-hearted as he clearly was, she had to admit that he was a handsome man.

Nothing about his hard, determined demeanor had really changed. She inclined her head and considered him again. No, maybe it had. She sensed another kind of distance about him, a new sort of remoteness. He felt even more unapproachable. And there was a decidedly weary edge about his posture.

She prayed that man hadn't told him more than he would say. If Danes already knew that her aunt was…hurt…

"Are you certain there isn't something you need to tell me?" she ventured.

"I've told you all there is to know."

He sounded tired rather than annoyed or impatient.

"I still don't like the idea of wasting the rest of the day. Shouldn't we be out looking? Isn't there something we can do?" It just felt wrong to wait while her aunt remained in the hands of a killer. She suppressed a shudder. What if the other man never called? How would she find her aunt then? She could be anywhere. Fear twisted inside her.

Danes pulled into the lot of a hotel, this one more upscale than the last. After parking in front of the lobby he sat silently for so long that Angel worried she'd pushed him too far. Anxiety sent her heart thumping against her rib cage. She should have kept her mouth shut. Another mistake. Would she never learn?

"Go in, get us a room." He handed her a credit card and driver's license. "Use that name."

"What?" He wanted her to go in alone? She had to have heard wrong.

"Just do it."

If the ferocity behind those three words hadn't been enough, the lethal look he pointed in her direction definitely did the trick. Angel wrenched the door open and hurried into the hotel lobby without hesitating. She glanced at the name on the credit card, then verified it with the name on the license before reaching the desk.

Damon Rodale. Cincinnati, Ohio.

"May I help you, ma'am?" The clerk gifted her with a practiced smile from behind his gleaming counter.

"Yes, I need a room." She placed the credit card and driver's license on the counter. "Just for one night," she added, producing a smile of her own.

The credit card was approved with a single swipe. No questions other than the usual, smoking or non-smoking, king or two double beds. Incredible. He recited the directions for the easiest access to the room and passed the key card along with the credit card and license across the counter.

"Thank you." She gathered the cards and fake ID but hesitated before leaving. "Do you have room service?" she asked, certain a hotel this size would.

"The kitchen is open until midnight," he assured with another gracious smile.

"Thank you."

Food entered the chaos in her head for the first time in more than twenty-four hours. She couldn't even remember the last time she'd eaten. Before she and Mildred had been descended upon by madmen? She was pretty sure that was correct. After she'd gotten her daughter safely tucked away she'd forced herself to eat in order to keep up her energy.

She wondered then when Danes had eaten last. She couldn't imagine him confessing to any sort of physiological need.

The sight of him sitting, his forehead braced against the steering wheel, struck her hard as she approached the vehicle.

She rushed to his door. "Are you all right?"

His head snapped upward at the same time his hand flew to his weapon with phenomenal speed. "Did you get the room?"

She nodded. "We can drive around back and park there. There's a rear exit near our room." It wasn't until she told him those details that she realized she should likely have asked for those very accommodations.

"Good."

As soon as she'd gotten in he pulled away from the parking slot and followed her instructions. She watched him closely as he walked to the hotel's rear entrance. His movements seemed steady but something was clearly wrong here. It wasn't until they were safely behind the locked door of their room that she knew just how wrong.

He winced as he removed his jacket. The tear in his black shirt and the slight variation in fabric color in the surrounding area loudly telegraphed the problem.

"You've been shot." She breathed the words.

He staggered but regained his balance with the aid of the nearest table. "I think I'm going to need your assistance."

"How bad is it?" She rushed to him and started to unbutton his shirt.

He manacled her hands in his. "No matter what happens," he warned, his voice taut, "don't take me to a hospital. We have to stay out of sight."

"But what if—"

He fell against her, his weight dragging them both down to the floor.

This time he didn't try to catch himself.

This time he didn't speak.

Chapter Seven

Lucas Camp sat down at the long conference table, alongside his wife. He didn't like the worry etched across her lovely face. He hadn't seen her this upset since before they'd discovered her son was alive.

When would this end?

"Still no word from Cole Danes?" she asked, her voice hollow from lack of sleep.

Lucas shook his head. "Nothing. I haven't been able to contact him since he left the office yesterday."

Victoria pressed her hands to her mouth.

"I know this is difficult, Victoria, but I still believe he will pull this off. He's never failed before. He won't this time."

She turned to him, anguish clouding her eyes. "How could this happen? Mildred…" She shook her head. "He may not be able to save Mildred and her niece. And, dear God, what about the child? Has anyone figured out where the child is?"

This hit far too close to home. Lucas hated to see her go through this kind of torment again. He'd sworn to protect her and he hadn't been able to. Leberman, the devil, still had his cronies. Lucas had a bad feeling that it wouldn't really be over until every last one of them was dead.

"I've got people working on it," he assured her gently. Never one to take chances, Lucas had two of his Specialists working the case. Unfortunately, Cole Danes had proven every bit as capable as his Specialists. He'd given them the slip as if they were mere recruits fresh out of training. But they would pick up his trail again. For now, Victoria didn't need to be bothered with any of that. "Casey believes Angel hid the child. That's why they've taken Mildred. It was the only other way they knew to get at Angel."

"What else does Casey have to say?"

Thomas Casey was Lucas's boss. The director of Mission Recovery and a good friend. He'd gone through this nightmare with Lucas, had provided unrelenting support. He had called this morning with an update he didn't want to discuss via the airwaves. His plane had arrived in Chicago thirty minutes ago. Lucas had sent a car to bring him to the office. Meanwhile, he and Victoria could only speculate as to what Casey had uncovered.

The door opened and Thomas Casey stepped inside the conference room. Lucas stood to greet him. Though nearly twenty years Lucas's junior, Thomas

Casey had amassed a wealth of experience in the world of covert operations. He was a top-notch director. But no one, not even Lucas, would ever know the man behind the job.

Thomas Casey didn't let anyone close.

"I apologize for being so vague when we spoke this morning," Casey said by way of greeting as he shook Lucas's outstretched hand. He nodded to Victoria. "Good to see you, Victoria."

"Thank you for coming. I hope you have some news that can help us, Thomas."

No one else in the world called Director Casey by his first name. Lucas suppressed a tiny smile. He doubted anyone other than Victoria would get away with it.

"I believe I have some insight that might be of use," he allowed.

"Why don't we sit." Lucas gestured to the chair directly across the table from where he and Victoria sat. "Coffee?"

"None for me, thanks." Casey settled into his chair.

Victoria shook her head when Lucas looked to her.

"Well then, let's get this thing started."

Casey set his briefcase on the table and opened it. He removed a manila folder marked classified and passed it to Lucas.

"I've looked a little more deeply into Cole Danes's past."

That news surprised Lucas. "His record is outstanding."

"That's true. Not a single failure." Casey leaned back in his chair. "Graduated from Yale with a law degree, went on to achieve his doctorate in foreign affairs. The man speaks a dozen different languages, even trained with Special Forces just to get the physical logistics right in case he needed them. He has negotiation and intimidation tactics down to a science. I'd like nothing better than to recruit him for my unit."

"So what else is new?" Lucas already knew all that. That's why he'd selected Danes for this assignment.

"Professionally he's something of a superhero," Casey agreed. "It's his personal life where things get complicated."

Lucas shrugged. "His father was an ambassador to an African country. He and his wife have since retired to Florida. One brother, six years older, who also worked for the State Department."

"Died in a car bombing in Libya fifteen years ago," Casey interjected.

"Not surprising," Lucas countered. "Libya's not exactly the place to be if you're American, not then, not now." Even with the new, so-called cooperation the Libyan government had shown lately, the country was still an unstable environment for Americans.

"One would think," Casey said mysteriously. "But

when I considered Danes's handling of the Howard Stephens case and then this latest turn of events, I took a closer look at his activities in the past ten or so years."

Lucas leaned forward to flip through the pages of the file Casey had brought.

"We know Errol Leberman and Howard Stephens formed an alliance. With a team of six men they carried out death warrants all over the world."

Again Lucas wondered what was new with that. "Go on," he prompted knowing Casey would not have come all this way without good reason which would include new information.

"I formulated a number of simulations," Casey explained. "I considered the deceased Danes son's work in international terrorism and the time frame. The man had quite a handle on the homeland terrorist situation even then. He made statements that our own worst enemies might come from within.

"If Cole Danes's beloved brother, his only sibling, had been murdered by homeland terrorists rather than foreigners that would make for excellent motivation for Danes to go after the culprits."

Lucas narrowed his gaze. "You're saying someone commissioned Leberman and Stephens to do the job and make it look 'work' related, as if his visit to Libya had been the reason he'd died."

"Right."

"But that's only speculation." Lucas flared his

hands skeptically. "I'll admit that after what's happened I considered the possibility that Danes had a personal stake in this, but there's no evidence to back it up."

"Maybe there is." Casey pointed to the file. "Check the dates. Until today, four of the six men Leberman and Stephens had recruited have been executed. We know this from what Victoria's son has related during the past few months."

Victoria shifted in her chair. "He hasn't remembered everything," she reminded. "There are a lot of holes in his memory."

"I understand that. But in each instance when one of Leberman's team was executed, there is documentation that Cole Danes was traveling in the area."

That got Lucas's attention. He shuffled through the pages. "You're certain." He didn't know why he asked. He knew Casey wouldn't introduce the scenario if he hadn't done his homework.

"Even when Leberman was here in Chicago, Danes was in the area. There's no evidence, of course, that he was involved in any way or made any sort of contact, but he was here."

Lucas sat back in his chair, a cold hard knot of apprehension forming in his gut. "So you think Danes is avenging his brother's death."

Casey nodded. "Not just his brother, his brother's wife and children, as well. Vengeance is the most likely scenario. Especially considering this morning's shoot-out. Another of the original six went down."

Lucas knew all about this morning's escapade. Chicago PD had related the story to Victoria when she called to inquire. One officer insisted that the EMTs had stated that Danes had questioned the shooting victim extensively before allowing him to be transported. The man had been DOA. Both EMTs had admitted that he would likely have died anyway. He'd lost a massive amount of blood, had serious internal injuries.

"That leaves only one," Victoria said, the worst-case scenario obviously taking shape for her, as well. She turned to Lucas. "My God," she murmured. "Surely he won't put his need for revenge ahead of Mildred's life."

Lucas wanted to reassure her…but he couldn't.

Considering this latest data, there was no way to know what Cole Danes would do.

"I will say this," Casey offered, dragging Lucas's attention back to him. "Cole Danes has a reputation for being fair as well as ruthless. Despite the scenario I've presented, we have every reason to believe he'll do the right thing. He always has."

Lucas hoped like hell he would do the right thing this time. He set his jaw hard. If Cole Danes allowed Mildred or Angel Parker to be hurt, Lucas would have no one to blame but himself for bringing the man into this situation. There was nothing he could

do to change that glaring fact, but he would make it
right on one level. It would be Cole Danes's first and
final mistake.

Chapter Eight

Renaissance Hotel, East Side of Chicago,
12:20 p.m.
21 hours, 55 minutes remaining...

There was no exit wound.

The bleeding had stopped but from what she could see Danes had already lost more blood than he should have. Too much for her comfort.

He lay on the bed now, a feat she would never have been able to accomplish alone. He'd roused enough to help, though she'd hated that his exerting any additional effort had been necessary.

"What're you waiting for?" His voice sounded sterner than it should for a man in his condition, but she didn't miss the thin quality. In the past twelve hours or so she'd come to know quite well the strong, rich sound.

She ordered her hands not to fidget and kept her gaze carefully away from his. "There's no exit wound."

"You'll find tweezers in the supplies I purchased. Dig it out."

Disregarding his suggestion, she looked around for any kind of distraction. "Have some ice chips." She'd called room service and ordered bottled water, crushed ice and coffee. She'd needed the caffeine, the rest had been for him. She'd cleansed the wound and surrounding area with bottled water and the peroxide he'd purchased. She'd also gone into the bathroom and made one other call...he wouldn't like it.

As hard as she tried her fingers still shook as she held a few chips of ice to his lips. He sucked them from her fingertips, the feel of his lips even under present circumstances sent an unexpected tingle through her.

She bit down on her lower lip and studied the small wound in his side as if considering his suggestion. There could be internal hemorrhaging. Experience told her that if the internal injuries were massive he'd be in shock by this point, suffering from extreme blood loss. But she couldn't be certain. Each individual's tolerance for pain and ability to function beyond normal limits was always different. He could be hanging by a thread, but his vitals were damn good if that turned out to be the case. His pulse was still strong, his heart rate very good considering.

"What have you done?"

Her head came up. "What do you mean?"

A knock at the door confirmed his suspicions. Why was it her luck never held out?

The weapon was in his hand before she realized his hand had moved. "That better be room service again."

She stood quickly and backed away from the bed. "I had to call a friend."

He pushed up into a sitting position. The grim line of his mouth exposed plainly how much the move cost him but he didn't make a sound in protest. "Don't answer it," he ordered, fury flashing in those eyes. "I don't want to have to kill anyone else this morning."

His words shook her but she refused to be intimidated on the issue. He needed more help than she could give. She was only a nurse, not a surgeon. "You don't have a choice." She strode to the door and reached for the knob. The sound of him chambering a round gave her only a second's pause; she twisted the knob and opened the door.

Keith Anderson smiled at her. "I was beginning to think you'd played some kind of joke on me," he said good-naturedly.

She pulled him into the room and quickly closed and locked the door. "Thanks for coming, Keith."

"Whoa! Who's the guy with the gun?"

Angel rolled her eyes and heaved a put-upon sigh. "Put the gun down, Danes. He's here to help."

Keith Anderson looked at her a little skeptically. "Are you in some kind of trouble?"

He'd asked that on the phone but she'd insisted

that there was no time to explain. She'd only known Keith a few months. He was friendly and flirtatious and currently in his surgical rotation. She'd warded off his friendly advances from day one. As nice as he was, as cute as he was, she'd learned the hard way not to date the doctors, med students or interns.

She grabbed him by the arm and pulled him closer to the bed. His hesitation was understandable since Danes refused to put his gun away.

"You brought what we need?" She glanced at the large shopping bag in his hand. She'd warned him not to *look* like a doctor, hence the casual attire and big brown paper bag.

A mixture of confusion and apprehension had claimed his face. "I brought what you asked for."

"Who the hell is this guy?" Danes demanded. His hair was loose now, hanging around his shoulders, the silver earring glinting in his earlobe. His black shirt ripped open, the leather shoulder holster still in place. She could well imagine what Keith thought.

"Keith Anderson. He's an intern at the hospital. He's going to help."

She looked away from Keith's questioning expression. He would want to know later, assuming either of them survived to see a later, why she'd lied. She saw him most every day at the hospital rightly enough, but he was only a fourth-year medical student. Still, he had three things going for him, he was in the final weeks of his surgery rotation, he was friendly and Angel knew she could trust him.

Danes's furious gaze locked onto hers. "Did you warn him that I'd have to kill him when he's through?"

"Put the gun away. We're wasting time," she ordered in the sternest tone she could marshal.

"Look, Angel." Keith backed away a step. "This is a little intense."

She seized his arm with both hands and waited until he'd looked at her before she spoke. "Please, Keith, this is important. I won't let him hurt you. Just do this for me, would you?"

He looked from her to the gun still aimed in his direction and back. "All right, but it's going to cost you." A wicked grin slid across his handsome face, outshining any of the other emotions still lingering there. "I won't let you forget it, either."

"Whatever you want," she promised.

Keith passed the bag to her and sat down on the edge of the bed, ignoring Danes's glare as well as his weapon. That was another thing she'd known about Keith. He would risk his standing at the hospital as well as the university to bring the necessary items. She doubted anyone else would have done that for her.

"Let me have a pair of those gloves," he mumbled to Angel, already distracted by the injury. He pulled a stethoscope from his jacket pocket.

Relief chased away the last of Angel's uncertainty. She handed him a pair of the gloves he'd brought and hurried to set up so she could assist him. She dragged the chair and table closer, then arranged the surgical equipment and medical supplies from the bag atop it.

"Let's get that IV going," Keith told her. His eyes told her he wasn't completely happy with the circumstances. She understood.

Angel donned a pair of gloves, took the necessary implements and moved to the other side of the bed. She draped the IV bag on the headboard and repeated, "Put the gun down, Danes."

He lowered the weapon to the mattress but didn't release it. When she pressed him with her gaze he said, "That's as good as it's going to get."

"Fine." She surveyed his forearm and decided on the best spot for the introduction of the IV catheter.

"What's in that?" He glanced toward the IV bag.

"Nothing to worry about," she assured, annoyed. The man needed help and all he could do was ask questions and complain. "You need the fluids, you've lost a lot of blood."

"No drugs?"

"No drugs yet, sir," Keith answered for her. "But you'll need something for this. It's going to be quite painful."

"No drugs." This time Danes directed his no-arguments order at Keith. "If I feel the first glimmer of an anesthetic you'll regret it."

Keith looked from Danes to Angel. "No way am I doing this without anesthesia."

Damn. "Did you bring a local?"

He shrugged. "Yeah, but—"

"Give him that."

"Angel, you—"

"Do it," Danes commanded. He repositioned the weapon on his right side, well within Keith's line of vision.

"Whatever."

Angel would not soon forget the next few minutes. The local helped somewhat, but not nearly enough. It was insane to do it this way, but Danes refused to allow any additional numbing drugs. To his credit, he didn't make a peep as Keith increased the size of the wound, then prodded with a pair of surgical retrieval forceps until he found the bullet lodged against a rib and removed it.

"Man, you were damn lucky," Keith said as he explored the area as best he could for any other damage. "A millimeter to the right and that sucker would have gone through your lung. As it is, you've got a fractured rib, but not a lot of other damage."

A fractured rib was no laughing matter. Angel scrubbed the back of a gloved hand over her forehead. She couldn't see how he'd withstood the pain for hours. They'd waited in that parking garage for what felt like forever, then purchased new clothes and come to this hotel. He'd driven, staying in complete control without so much as flinching. Amazing. She refused to consider that the bullet he'd taken had been as much to protect her as to help himself.

As far as she was concerned at this moment, he didn't deserve quite that much respect or gratitude just yet.

As any good nurse would do, she wiped his face with a cool cloth, his sweat the only outward indication of what he'd just endured.

"I'll get this sutured and then you'll need an injection of penicillin. That drug acceptable?" Keith inquired facetiously.

Danes lifted the corners of his mouth in a facsimile of a smile. "That and nothing else."

Angel rolled her eyes again. She had no desire to watch this part. The local was surely wearing off by now. She busied herself cleaning up the remnants of the crude procedure. Using a trash bag from one of the lined cans in the room she concealed the contents by tying the bag. She doubted Danes would want anyone to know surgery to remove a bullet had taken place in this room. There wasn't much she could do about the bloody towels except trash them, too.

"Looks like you'll live."

As she moved back into the room Keith stood and gathered the remainder of the items he'd brought. He'd bandaged the wound and injected the antibiotic.

"I suppose I'll allow you to do the same," Danes offered with something less than civility.

"I really appreciate your help, Keith." Angel followed him to the door. "I know this was…" She couldn't think of any words to put the situation into proper context.

Keith tugged her into the corridor and pulled the door closed behind them. "Look, are you sure you're okay? What's going on here?"

For a guy so young, with mostly medicine and sex on his mind, Keith looked dead serious and immensely worried.

"I can't tell you anything more now." She placed her hand over his. "I promise I'll explain everything later."

He shook his head. "But this guy. He's—"

"Helping me," she finished. "I can't do this without him. Trust me, Keith, I'm doing what I have to."

"All right." He brushed a kiss across her forehead. "Be safe. I plan to collect on this debt."

Angel couldn't say what possessed her at that moment, but she flung her arms around the handsome young doctor-to-be's neck and kissed him hard right on the mouth. She couldn't help herself. The desperation, the need to connect with another living human was too great to ignore. And the last thing she intended to do was let that need get out of control with no one around except Cole Danes.

Maybe this kiss really did belong to him, but he wasn't going to get it.

"Well now, that's what I call tangible appreciation," Keith murmured when at last they came up for air. He kissed the tip of her nose. "Be safe. I'd like to follow up on this procedure, nurse."

Trembling with the sudden drain of adrenaline, she watched him walk out the rear exit of the hotel. A part of her now certain that she'd lost her mind completely. She'd just kissed the cutest, sexiest, most available male medical student at Winnetka General. And she hadn't felt a thing—except desperation.

Maybe she was already dead.

Any woman who could kiss a guy like that and feel empty afterward had to be dead.

She trudged back into the room, certain her past experience with one particular doctor was surely the reason for her lack of physical reaction. One look at Cole Danes and she knew it was a lie.

"What the hell are you doing?"

He'd holstered his weapon and managed to get out of bed. The grim, listless expression on his face served as irrefutable proof of the discomfort involved.

"Get your things. We're out of here."

He ripped off the tape and removed the IV catheter to reiterate his announcement.

"Now," he added, just in case she still didn't get it.

She flung her arms heavenward in disbelief. "Are you nuts? You should be in bed for at least twenty-four hours. There could be other problems. God forbid, an aneurysm related to the injury. Or infection."

And then it hit her. In less than twenty-four hours her aunt would be dead if they didn't find her. Her child might be lost to her forever. Danes wasn't willing to risk any outside interference, not that she believed Keith would call the authorities, but it was a risk. Not to mention, even she had already learned that staying in one place any longer than necessary was a risk in and of itself.

She wilted. Any strength and determination flowing out of her so fast she scarcely stayed on her feet.

"You'll drive."

Her hands trembling, she pushed the hair behind her ears and nodded. "Okay." She gathered the new clothes he'd purchased and the toiletries before heading for the door.

She hesitated there, had to ask the question that now burned like a wildfire in her brain. "Do you think he'll call?" If he didn't…what would they do? How would they find her aunt in time?

Danes looked tired, the pain no longer hidden. The lines drawn by the fatigue and pain added a new dimension to his face. Made her see more than the classically handsome angles good DNA had provided. Yet his eyes revealed the most. Despite the physical discomfort, this man was stronger than anyone she'd met in her life. He would not stop, would not give up…and that gave her hope in the midst of her mounting despair.

"He'll call."

Again some renegade brain cell took control of her determination to maintain distance, both physical and emotional, between them. "Thank you," she whispered, her emotions too raw to manage anything more than a murmur. She would never forget the way he'd thrown her to the ground and covered her with his own body, then ushered her beneath that car while the bullets hissed around him. "For saving my life this morning."

"Don't thank me yet."

Blue Moon Motel, outside Chicago, 4:15 p.m.
18 hours remaining…

ANGEL AWOKE WITH A START. The room was dark. She blinked. Where was she?

Then she remembered.

The shooting. The makeshift surgery.

Danes had instructed her to drive here. Too exhausted to fight the need then, she'd slept. She dreamed of her sweet little girl, of how their life used to be before evil had intruded. Then the nightmare had begun.

She sat up now and listened.

Where was Danes?

The sound of running water drew her gaze toward the bathroom. Light spilled from beneath the closed door. He must have decided to risk leaving her alone long enough for a shower himself. As if she would make a run for it? What would she do then? Her only option was to stay with him and pray he knew what he was doing.

Why hadn't the man called?

She switched on the bedside lamp and crawled off the bed. Curling up in a chair near the window, she fished around in her purse for her cell phone. He'd turned it off again.

She turned it on and checked her voice messages. Nothing.

How was the call supposed to come with the phone turned off? His cutting remark that the cell phone could be used to track their whereabouts flitted through her mind. But that was only after a call had actually connected, right?

She shoved the hair back from her face and tried to reason the best course of action. Leave it on or turn it back off?

The blast of chimes as it rang made her jump. She almost dropped the phone. It took a second for her to catch her breath as well as her wits to answer it.

"Don't answer it."

Her thumb froze on the button, the desire to press downward a near palpable force.

"It's him." She recognized the jumble of numbers and letters. Danes had explained that the untraceable characters meant nothing. The call couldn't be traced and couldn't be called back.

"Put the phone down."

He stood just outside the bathroom door. She could answer it before he reached her. He didn't have his gun or his holster. A loosely tied towel hung around his lean hips. A fresh, dry bandage covered his recent injury but his damp hair told her he'd only just emerged from the shower.

The burst of melodious notes crackled in the dead air between them, urging her to respond.

"We're running out of time," she pleaded. "Please, I have to answer."

"No."

There was no hesitation, not the slightest inkling of uncertainty in his expression or his voice.

What did she do?

Trust this man's judgment? A stranger who'd alternately treated her like a criminal and saved her life?

"He'll call again, then you'll answer."

A third ring rent the air.

"How can you be so sure?"

"I know what he wants. He won't stop until he has it."

Maybe it was the soft, however deadly quality of his voice, or maybe it was the sheer determination in those penetrating blue eyes. Whatever motivated her, Angel had to believe. Had to hang on to something…anything. And he was all she had.

She set the phone on the table next to her purse. Two more urgent rings and silence filled the room once more.

Her gaze moved to latch on to his. All signs of fatigue and pain had vanished along with the stubble on his jaw. He looked ready for anything, including her protests. He needn't worry, she had no energy to argue. She moved back to the bed and drew her knees up to her chest. She didn't want to be near the phone, wasn't sure she could resist answering it if it rang again.

She closed her eyes and fought a wave of fierce emotion. Defeat conquered any remaining determination. They were running out of time and she was completely lost as to what to do. Every fiber of her being screamed at her to do something, yet, in her heart she feared that nothing she did would matter. That this would not have a happy ending no matter what anyone did.

The scrape of fabric skimming flesh followed by the metal on metal grind of a fly closing registered his continued presence in the room. She could only hope that he had a plan and was getting dressed in preparation for carrying it out.

She felt the mattress shift, smelled the scent of soap, the one the motel provided, the same one she'd used. Instantly the image of him gliding that small bar over his skin evolved in her mind.

"This is difficult, I know."

She lifted her gaze to his. Her eyes stung with the tears she could no longer hold at bay. "I just want my life back. I want my baby back home. I want my aunt safe."

For the first time since he'd barged into this whole crazy mess he touched her in a way not meant to restrain. He tucked her hair behind her ear so gently her breath trapped in her chest. That he could be so gentle startled her. But it was his eyes that did the most damage to her already strained and raw emotions. The intensity she fully recognized, the feral determination as familiar as his face and name had become. It was the one alien element that shook her as nothing else could have.

Need.

Absolute, infinite.

"Tell me about your daughter."

The request surprised her all over again. Did he really want to know, or was this some method of distracting her so she wouldn't go off the deep end looming entirely too close?

"Her name is Mia." Angel smiled as she thought of her sweet baby. "After my mom."

"Where is she?"

Warning bells jangled in her brain. "Why do you want to know?"

He studied her closely for a moment before he answered. "Someone from the Colby Agency could see that she is safe."

Her hackles rose. "I already know she's safe. Months of research went into my decision," she said tightly. "Like you, I didn't want to take any chances."

"Fair enough."

The hint of amusement in his expression only made her more furious. "Just because you don't care about anyone that much doesn't mean everyone looks at life through those jaded lenses."

The amusement vanished. "I'm not jaded, Miss Parker. I'm simply focused."

She huffed a skeptical breath. "That's just an excuse not to let anyone close to you, *Mr. Danes.* There are lots of people who are focused without being so…" She frowned as she searched for the right word. "Untouchable. It's not natural to be so far removed from life. You have to trust someone sometime. Have to take a chance."

"Like the one you took four years ago?"

His barb had the intended effect. The old hurt twisted deeply through her. "Yeah," she admitted, though she'd have preferred to tell him where to go and how to get there. "Exactly like that. I trusted him. Even stupidly fell in love." She looked straight into those piecing eyes. "And I don't regret it. I have my daughter because of that relationship."

She'd been in her last year of nursing school. He'd been an intern at the hospital where she took her training. The relationship had been over as fast and furiously as it began, but she would never regret it. Sure the guy had been a jerk. He'd wanted no part of a child, had never called even once since moving away. But Angel didn't care. She loved her daughter.

"She looks like you."

Danes's comment drew her back to the present.

She nodded. Though she didn't hate the guy who'd fathered her child, she was thankful her daughter didn't look like him. Mia had the same blond hair and pale blue eyes as Angel. Not a speck of Dr. No-Strings showed through.

"But I'll have to tell her about him sometime," she said more to herself than to the man sitting next to her. She wasn't sure why she'd said it out loud but there it was.

"He has no interest in the child?"

She couldn't help smiling. What was with Danes tonight? He was full of surprises.

"I imagine you know the answer to that already." She felt confident he'd thoroughly investigated her past.

The barest hint of a smile twitched one corner of his mouth and her heart surged at the sight. She was hopeless. She'd been sure that kiss she'd laid on Keith and then the long hot shower and couple hours of sleep would clear her head. Evidently it hadn't.

Cole Danes might be totally ruthless but he was undeniably appealing on a wholly physical level. No way could she ignore that fact a moment longer. It had to be the stress. Had to be that crazy connection people shared when under extreme pressure.

Like now.

"You think you've got me all figured out," he proposed, that voice silky, sexy and way too deep and rich for comfort.

Why pretend? He'd read her already, knew exactly what was on her mind.

She shrugged, shook her head. "I wouldn't presume to understand a man as complicated as you," she admitted. "It's me that I'm having trouble with."

His gaze latched on to hers and for one mad moment she was certain he would kiss her. Crazy. The worst possible thing that could happen. And yet she wanted it more than she wanted to draw her next breath.

The tinny chime of her cell phone shattered the air.

Danes looked away first.

Angel didn't have to move…didn't have to look at the caller ID.

It would be *him*.

Chapter Nine

"What am I supposed to say?" Angel's heart pumped frantically. The passage of time abruptly pressed in on her once more. She'd lost track there for a moment. Foolishly. They should have been planning some sort of maneuver…some strategy.

Danes extended his hand toward her, the cell phone lying in his palm. "Start with hello."

Another barrage of musical notes punctured her composure. She moistened her lips, exhaled an unsteady breath and reached for the one connection between her and the man holding her aunt for ransom.

"Hello."

"Where is Danes?" the harsh voice demanded.

"He…he's right here." Her gaze locked with the one watching her so very intently.

"You tell that son of a bitch he's mine."

Danes snatched the phone away from her and severed the connection. Stunned, she at first thought he'd reacted to her mushrooming panic but that wasn't the case at all.

"What did you do that for? He didn't have time to tell me what to do next?"

"When he calls back," Danes began, "I want—"

"Are you crazy?" She grabbed for the phone. "Time is almost up. I have to know what he wants us to do next!"

"When he calls back," Danes repeated, his voice cool, calm, patient, "I want you to tell him I won't let you talk to him anymore. That I'm through playing games. Before I end the call again you shout out that the other man told me what I needed to know."

She blinked. "He told you what?" Why hadn't he said anything? Why hadn't they already rescued her aunt if he knew *everything?*

"It's imperative that you do exactly as I say."

"Wait a minute." She shot up off the bed, planted her hands on her hips and glared down at him. "You mean to tell me you know where my aunt is? If you've been keeping that from me—"

The telephone jingled, cutting off the rest of her intended threat.

"Do exactly as I said," he reminded before handing the phone back to her.

She wanted to hurt him. The need overwhelmed all other emotions. She punched the talk button. "He won't let me talk to you," she blurted.

"Then your aunt—"

Danes snatched the phone from her hand and gave her a prompting nod.

"He already knows everything!" she cried. "Your friend told him everything before—"

Danes ended the call. "Very good."

Angel sagged down onto the mattress, the barrage of emotion too heavy to bear. "Please, just tell me the truth. I need to know she's going to be all right."

She would not cry. Damn him. She looked at the clock and fought another wave of emotion. Only seventeen hours left. They had to do something.

Danes pushed to his feet and for a while she feared he wouldn't bother to answer. Would simply ignore her plea. Then he looked down at her with something like compassion in his eyes. But it couldn't have been that simple, she knew all too well. Cole Danes felt nothing for anyone. Yes, there might be a physical spark between them, but that was it.

He would never allow anything more.

"It's me he wants. As long as he needs your aunt to lure me in, she'll be safe."

"Is that supposed to make me feel better?" She lunged upward, matched his stance. "How is he supposed to lure you in when you won't let me talk to him?" God, she couldn't believe she was asking that. Now who lacked compassion?

"We should get started."

Angel rubbed her eyes and shook her head. This

whole thing grew more and more insane with each passing moment. "You're hurt, you shouldn't be doing anything but resting." Her voice sounded as hollow as she felt. Nothing made sense anymore. She didn't know what to believe, or what to hope for. If she prayed for her aunt's survival, did that mean Danes was to die?

What did that make her?

What would Mildred do in her shoes?

And suddenly Angel knew. Mildred would be strong. She would do whatever necessary to accomplish her goal.

"The pain is tolerable," he stated matter-of-factly. "I'll be fine."

"Do you need me to drive?" She gathered her purse, dropped the cell phone into it.

"That would be helpful." He pulled on his jacket. From the corner of her eye she saw him wince.

She nodded and followed him out the door. However stoic he appeared, she knew he suffered. Though the injury mostly involved tissue, no major damage other than the cracked rib, there would be pain associated with that as well as the sutures. Since he refused to take any sort of pain reliever, he had to be working hard to tune out the pain. Weakness as a result of the blood loss was likely taking its toll. She'd have to keep an eye on him.

For the first time since she'd encountered Cole Danes she wondered what drove him? Why was he doing this? She knew full well how important Mildred was to Victoria Colby-Camp and the Colby Agency. Was Danes doing the job he'd been hired by Victoria to do or was there something more here? Something she didn't fully understand.

She sensed there was. But how in the world could she possibly hope to learn the secrets of a man like Cole Danes?

COLE DIRECTED HER to the temporary apartment he'd moved into while working on the Colby Agency investigation. Only a few blocks off the Magnificent Mile and from the Colby Agency offices, the luxurious high-rise had offered nothing more than a place to sleep and change clothes.

"Mr. Danes, how are you this evening?" the uniformed doorman asked as Cole approached the door.

"Fine, thank you, Metcalf."

The doorman, one of four employed by the building, nodded to Angel. She smiled awkwardly, hesitated as if not sure what to say or do. Cole ushered her into the lobby and toward the elevator.

"Where are we?" she whispered when they were out of earshot of the doorman.

"My place."

He almost smiled at her surprised look. He'd learned that about her in the past few hours. She wasn't very good at disguising her emotions, was a hideous liar. Just another of those little things that made her far too innocent to be involved with men like Leberman and Stephens and their cronies.

With men like him for that matter.

In the elevator he selected his floor, ten, and waited impatiently for the doors to close and the car to glide upward.

"I guess you make a lot of money in your line of work," she ventured. "Much more than a nurse." She smiled shyly.

That smile, though chock-full of trepidation, disturbed him somehow. He didn't understand it, didn't even try. He could only reason that lack of sleep and physical discomfort were playing havoc with his ability to think clearly. He had to focus.

"More than a nurse most likely," he agreed, though he kept his gaze focused anywhere but upon her. The clothes they'd purchased fit differently from the ones she'd been wearing before. Tighter perhaps, more formfitting certainly. Under other circumstances he would have considered the possibility as a ploy to distract him, but the selections had been hurried at best. Perhaps he hadn't really noticed the finer details of her figure previously.

He shouldn't notice now.

That he did provided ample evidence of his inability to stay focused.

"Wow."

He'd scarcely opened the door and turned on the lights and already she moved around the living room, admiring the decorating and furnishings. None of which had anything to do with him. The place had come furnished.

There was no time to waste giving her a personal tour. He'd barely seen the place himself. In reality, elegance was something he'd come to take for granted. Money could buy most anything and that was a luxury he'd never been without.

The supplies he needed for tonight were stowed in the bedroom closet. He selected carefully and packed the items in a backpack. He straightened, hauling the heavy pack onto his shoulder, a stab of pain cut through his gut.

A line of sweat instantly popped out along his forehead. Getting shot hadn't been part of the plan, but it was a deviation he could deal with. In the en suite bathroom he swallowed a couple of over-the-counter pain relievers and washed them down with a gulp of water. That would have to get him through the night.

Time was too short to allow anything to slow down his responses.

He found Angel in the kitchen.

"Your cupboards are bare," she said jokingly, though he sensed that it wasn't actually a joke.

"You're hungry?"

"Starved. I hadn't even thought about it until a little while ago." She glanced at the digital clock on the microwave. "But the time is going by so fast." Her worried gaze bumped back into his. "What do we do now?"

"Now we get you some food."

They exited the building and, with her at the wheel of the rented car, he directed her to a drive-thru restaurant. Sub sandwiches and soft drinks were fast and easy. Food would help fuel him, as well. Though he rarely bothered to slow down long enough to eat when on an investigation. The injury added another demand on him physically. Food would be helpful.

In deference to the time, they ate en route. Occupied with the food and following his instructions, she didn't ask about the final destination until they'd parked in the quiet Chicago Heights neighborhood.

"Where are we?" she asked. She'd polished off her sandwich. The lady had definitely been famished.

"At the home of one of the EMTs."

"Why?"

"Because our friend will want to know what I learned from his fallen comrade."

Even in the dark, fear glittered visibly in her wide eyes. "What did you learn?"

"That's not important at the moment."

When she would have argued, he cut in smoothly, "We have to go inside his house and set up our surveillance."

"We're going to break into his house?"

Clearly the EMT wasn't home. The house was dark. And Cole already knew that the man volunteered at a local soup kitchen two nights per week, this being one of them.

"How do you know he'll come here? Weren't there two EMTs?"

Very good. He liked that she could think beyond the moment.

"The other EMT is pulling an extra shift tonight. He'll be the easiest to locate."

"How do you know that?"

"I made a few calls while you were sleeping." He'd asked after both EMTs and the dispatcher had happily given him all the information he requested. Of course, the fact that he'd introduced himself as a federal agent had helped. He theorized that their target would do the same.

"What if the first EMT tells him all he needs to know?"

"He can't, he wasn't close enough to hear."

She appeared to accept that explanation.

"I've never broken into anyone's house before," she admitted.

But then he knew that. Angel Parker had never been in trouble in her life until Howard Stephens appeared. She'd just been a typical single parent attempting to survive despite being overworked and underpaid.

She would never be typical again. Her life was forever changed.

For the first time in a very long time, Cole wished he possessed the power to right someone else's wrong. He'd been so focused the past ten years he hadn't taken the time to wonder or even to care what happened to anyone else. He had his own demons. But now, sitting in the dark, outside a stranger's house, he truly wished he could make all of this go away for this young woman.

But he couldn't.

He had to finish this.

And nothing, not even this innocent woman, would get in his way.

Angel followed Danes through the darkness. The last time she'd looked at the clock she'd had to fight off a tidal wave of fresh fear. Barely fourteen hours left. It felt as if they were no closer now than they'd been this time last night. It seemed impossible that she'd already spent more than twenty-four hours with Danes.

Strangely it felt like a lot longer. Like a minieternity. All the while bouncing from one extreme to the other. One minute she hated him and the next she wanted to touch him as, apparently, no one else ever had.

She couldn't think about anything else right now. Her aunt's life hung in the balance. She hadn't seen her daughter in days. And she was so tired. Those few hours of sleep had done little to ward off her bone-deep fatigue.

She could only image how Danes felt. He hadn't

slept at all as far as she could tell. The pain had to be a constant nag. But it didn't slow him. For that she was thankful. If he could help her aunt, she'd follow him most anywhere.

He withdrew a small tool from his shoulder pack and in seconds was inside the back door of the tiny cottage. The man could do anything it seemed.

She shivered at the thought of what kind of lover he would make. Would he be as brutal in bed as he was on the job? Why was she even thinking about that? Now of all times? The whole idea was far too ludicrous to even consider.

You are truly out of your mind, Angel.

Her cheeks flushed when she thought of how she'd kissed Keith Anderson today. He had to think she'd lost it completely. The guy had been after her for weeks—months—for a date. If she survived this, she would never keep him at bay now. Maybe it wouldn't be so awful if she hadn't been obsessing about Danes. He was the one she'd wanted to kiss. Stupid. Stupid.

How could she want to kiss a man who'd been nothing short of mean to her? Okay, he had saved her life. But he was…rude and grouchy. He barely showed any emotion. The whole concept was nuts.

But then, she could pick 'em, couldn't she? She'd fallen head over heels for the father of her child and what had that gotten her? The child she loved, yes, but a broken heart, too. She'd promised herself not to fall for another guy she couldn't read…couldn't trust.

Cole Danes was impossible to read and trusting him was emotional suicide.

But he was all she had in this.

She watched him move about the dark house with nothing but a flashlight to guide him. His movements were smooth, his gait as sleek as a cat's. Not once had he bumped into anything. She didn't dare move for fear of knocking something over. He was completely at home in the dark.

His clothes blended perfectly with the night. Black shirt, black slacks. He probably wore black briefs or boxers, as well.

She thought about the way he'd looked when he come out of the bathroom wearing only a towel. His skin was as smooth and sleek as his movements. Stretched tight over ridges of muscle that made her mouth dry just remembering them. As strong as he was, as well-defined as his muscles were, he looked lean and hard, not an ounce of fat or unnecessary bulge of muscle. She doubted anything about this man went to waste. Unlike other humans he didn't waste energy on emotion. That ability made him immune to the hurts of everyday life.

What kind of childhood environment or event in his life had made him that way? At forty, he should be married, should have kids. But he didn't. He claimed he didn't have anyone. What about parents, brothers or sisters? Surely he had loved his family.

He evidently had money, seemed accustomed to its availability. Had he been born to wealth or was he a self-made man?

"Now we wait."

She jerked at the sound of his voice right next to her. "You're through?"

"Yes."

She'd been lost in an imaginary episode of Cole Danes. Had lost all sense of the here and now. "We wait in here?"

"In the car. I'll monitor the house from there."

"Good." She didn't know what else to say. Still had no clue what he had planned.

Sensing that he didn't want anyone to hear them she kept her questions to herself until they were safely settled back into the car. He took the passenger seat so she slid back behind the steering wheel.

He placed a small black box on the dash and tinkered with it for a bit, all without the aid of light.

She couldn't wait to see if he could leap tall buildings in a single bound. He'd taken a bullet without much more than a blink.

So this was what action heroes were like. Extremely intelligent, relentless, but sadly lacking in the personality department.

Too bad.

She had to think about something else. She

couldn't stand sitting here in the dark in shocking silence. Thinking about him…not thinking—obsessing.

She'd gotten up to the three digits when he asked, "Do you always count stars when you're nervous?"

She relaxed into the seat and folded her arms over her breasts. "I wasn't counting stars," she lied. "I was…" What? "Checking out the constellations."

He made a little sound, a kind of breathy chuckle. It surprised her so that she had to look at him.

"You have something to say?"

She couldn't believe she'd asked that…couldn't believe any of this was happening.

What had she done to anger the universe? Her aunt had been kidnapped. Her daughter in the care of strangers. And here she was chatting about the constellations with a man she'd only met twenty-four hours ago and who had threatened to kill her at least once.

But he did save your life, a little voice reminded.

"Tell me about you and Mr. Anderson."

His question startled her from her confusing thoughts.

"Keith?"

"Yes. The gentleman who kindly stitched me up."

"I see him at the hospital."

"I know that part. What about the rest?"

She frowned, irritation drawing a line between her eyebrows. "We're friends, if that's what you mean."

"Maybe from your perspective," he said off-handedly.

Why the hell were they talking about this?

"Excuse me, can you tell me what we're waiting for here?" She plopped her hands out in a what-the-hell gesture. "You haven't told me anything."

She had to get back on track. She closed her eyes and ordered herself to calm down.

"We're waiting for our EMT to come home. My guess is our target will soon follow."

"Then what?" He never told her everything. Never. He'd give her so much and then nothing!

"Then we take it from there. Our move depends upon what he says and does."

The epiphany struck her like an electrical charge from a cardiac defibrillator. "You don't know anything, do you? That dying man didn't…Oh God." He couldn't rescue her aunt because he didn't know anything. That's why they were sitting in the dark waiting for the EMT to show…hoping the target, as he called him, fell into the trap.

"I know enough," Danes said as he surveyed the still-dark house.

She grabbed his shirtsleeve, demanding his full attention. "Why didn't you let me talk to him? He would have told us what he wanted us to do next!"

If Danes played out this stupid scenario and her aunt was harmed in any way—

He manacled her wrist and jerked her close. "This

isn't about what he wants," he growled savagely. "This is about staying one step ahead, leading the game instead of following."

"This isn't a game," she cried softly.

"It's been a game from the very beginning," he argued, some of the conviction seeping from his harsh tone. "That's what men like Howard Stephens and Errol Leberman do. They play games with life and death. It's who they are."

She swallowed at the panic crowding into her throat. "And is that who you are?" She blinked back the sting of tears. Dammit, she would not cry. Not now.

Her eyes had long ago adjusted to the dark night, allowing her to make out the details of his face in the light from the low-slung moon and brilliant stars. His gaze dropped to her lips and she trembled. Foolish, foolish, but she simply could not suppress the reaction.

"I don't play games, Angel," he murmured. The sound of her name on his lips sent another shiver racing through her.

"Just promise me that you won't let anything happen to my aunt. I need to know that this is going to be okay. I don't think I can keep it together much longer without something to hang on to."

"I'll do everything I can to keep her safe, but I can't guarantee you that he hasn't hurt her already."

A sob quaked through her in spite of her best efforts to hold it back.

"But I can promise you that this nightmare will soon be over. He will die."

Again the idea that this was more than just a job prodded at her. This was personal somehow. She could feel it. Could feel his hatred. She had no idea where he'd come from or how he fit into this. All she knew was that the Colby Agency had hired him to find the leak. But there had to be more.

"Who are you?"

"It doesn't matter." He released her and turned his attention back to the house.

Angel thought about that for a time. She mulled over the mistakes she'd made in her own life. How she'd mourned the loss of her parents. They'd been ripped from her life in an instant by a drunk driver. She closed her eyes and pushed away the memories of that night. Her aunt had brought her the news in person, not wanting her to learn from anyone else or over the phone. She'd been there for Angel ever since.

A part of her would always be convinced that the sudden, unbearable loss had caused her to seek solace in all the wrong places. First by driving herself too hard in her studies. It sounded like a worthy cause, but she'd ended up run-down physically and with a case of the flu she'd had a hell of a time shaking. Then she'd turned to other interests, like her sorely lacking social life. The next thing she knew she'd fallen for the wrong guy and ended up pregnant.

Once again, her aunt had been there to pick up the pieces. Her daughter had become the center of her life as well as her aunt's. Life had felt pretty close to perfect for a little while.

Then that evil man had shown up at her door, had taken her child just to prove he could. He had forced her to do things that would ultimately hurt her aunt. There had been nothing else she could do. At least she'd thought so at the time.

Had she been wrong?

Could she have made different decisions?

She just couldn't risk her daughter's safety. That was the bottom line. She had done whatever necessary to keep her safe.

Isn't that what all parents did?

Once you had a child, everything changed. Nothing else in the world mattered as much.

Without reservation she knew that her aunt understood and would have made the same choices herself. That was the one part in all of this that she felt absolutely certain of.

Still, with all she'd learned in church all those Sundays as a child, with every fiber of her being, she knew that what she'd done was wrong.

And now she had to face the consequences. She had to do whatever it took to save her aunt.

Her gaze drifted back to Cole Danes.

His need to do this was every bit as strong as hers. She could feel the rightness of that conclusion in the deepest recesses of her soul. But why? What had driven him to this point? To this terrible place?

"Tell me," she said, her voice sounding stark after the long minutes of silence. Danes turned to look at her, his expression utterly void of emotion. But there was something there, something she just couldn't see. The intensity of it reached out to her on a level far beyond words. "What did he do to you?"

Chapter Ten

The question echoed in Cole's brain. *What did he do to you?*

He stared out into the night, torn by the woman more than the question. How was it that she had penetrated his defenses so easily? In more than a decade no one had held the power to make him feel uncertain…until now.

"I know there's something," she pressed. "This is as personal to you as it is to me. You know all there is to know about me. Why can't I at least know this about you?"

Such a simple question.

And yet more complicated than she could possibly fathom.

Years of pent-up emotions churned inside him, dwarfing the nagging pain in his side.

"What makes you think I know all there is to

know about you?" he asked, changing the course of the conversation.

Soon the EMT would arrive and there would be no more time for talk.

"Wait a minute," she argued with a husky laugh. "The question was about you, not me."

The uproar inside him instantly began to settle at the sound of her voice, soft and fragile, yet immensely warm. This was the first time he'd heard her laugh. He liked it. Full, rich, not that silly tinkling sound most women made. Coming from such a slender, vulnerable-looking waif it took him entirely by surprise.

He swung his gaze to hers. "I didn't know about Dr. Anderson."

"Please," she protested with a dramatic roll of those lovely eyes. "I told you, we're friends. And, to be honest with you, he's not even a doctor. He's a med student." At his skeptical look she quickly added, "But he is in his surgery rotation. And we are only friends."

"Not from the gentleman's perspective." Keith Anderson wanted her. His interest was quite clear. Somehow that realization had disturbed Cole. Ridiculous, he knew, but true. He didn't like the way the young man looked at her. Admittedly, Anderson's age and occupation were more suitable. Cole was much too old, his work far too dangerous.

What the hell was he thinking?

"Cole…" A little hitch in her breathing, the one that unsettled him so unreasonably, disrupted her intake of breath. "I'm sorry. Danes," she amended.

The pause that followed went unanswered. He knew what she wanted. Proper etiquette insisted that he assure her that she could call him by his first name if she liked. But Cole had never been one to adhere to anyone's etiquette.

"I made it a rule a long time ago," she went on despite his flagrant snub, "not to get involved with anyone at work. I learned the hard way that things aren't always what they seem."

She didn't say more but she didn't have to. As she'd alluded, he already knew most everything. She rarely dated and nothing came of the few efforts at socializing she'd attempted since her child came into her life. Cole suspected she either had a problem committing or hadn't met anyone interested in a ready-made family.

"My daughter is the top priority in my life," she noted aloud, confirming his conclusions. "I can't imagine my life without her."

Something about the way she said that last statement drew his eyes back to her. So damn young, barely twenty-five. A three-year-old daughter and all alone, except for the aunt she adored.

Cole swallowed at the uncharacteristic lump of emotion clogging his throat. How was it a woman so seemingly fragile survived in such a tough world. Especially when faced with men like Howard Stephens and Errol Leberman. He couldn't imagine the fortitude and courage required coming from someone so young and inexperienced.

Angel Parker had no idea just how cruel the world could be. She had not and likely would not ever know the harsh realities he had looked dead in the eye. She could not possibly imagine what Stephens and Leberman were truly capable of. Her experiences had merely scratched the surface. And yet, here she sat fully prepared to do whatever it took, to face anything necessary to keep her aunt from harm.

"You have no idea the level of danger you are in at this very moment," he offered, unable to hold back the words.

She blinked those long lashes a couple of times to disguise the fear that flickered in her eyes, but he saw it just the same. "Yes, I do. That's why I bought the gun. I was afraid…I knew I couldn't do this without help." She stared down at her hands, her fingers twisted together nervously. "I don't want to be a victim anymore. I want this over."

That was just it. No one wanted to be a victim.

But every day, every hour, every damn second of each minute, someone became a victim in one way or another. The only way not to be a victim was to do as he had. No attachments. No close contact on a personal level at all. Complete focus on one's mission. Nothing else. Even basic human compassion was a weakness.

People like Angel Parker weren't built with the necessary equipment to turn everything and everyone off. For that very reason, she would always be susceptible.

Not like him.

If he died this second no one would care. He doubted if even his parents would mourn the loss of the son they'd actually lost ten years ago. They had grieved for one son. Cole had ensured that they would not grieve for another. He'd taken himself out of the equation, lived for only one purpose.

Revenge.

He had not confessed that truth to anyone, not even himself until now. His father had realized the task he'd taken on and that was part of what kept Cole away.

The irony was that here, in the darkness, a fragile woman he'd only just met, made him feel the one thing he'd sworn never again to suffer.

Need.

An error of monumental proportions.

Her life, the life of her aunt, depended upon his ability to do what he did best.

Forge ahead without distraction, without care for anyone or anything else.

Somehow, in the past few hours, a seemingly insignificant space in time, she'd taken that advantage away from him.

And he had no idea how to get it back.

For the first time in more than a decade, the vaguest glimmer of uncertainty crept into the cold, unfeeling pump that pulsed in his chest.

He almost laughed. His punishment, he concluded. God had taken his time, but the moment had finally come. Cole Danes would now stand in judgment for all his cruelties. For his lack of compassion, for his relentless determination to rid this world of scum like Stephens at any cost.

A hell of a time to reap what he'd sown.

The most amusing part was that he'd stopped believing in God about the same time a vital element had gone missing in his damaged heart. Accountability. Another human weakness he had triumphed over. Yet even he had to admit that his current predicament was far too ironic to be the result of mere fate.

Just his luck.

Cole reached into the glove box and withdrew the compact 9mm he'd taken from her that first night. "Keep the safety on until you're prepared to shoot."

She accepted the weight of the weapon into her small, delicate hands. A deep, ragged breath accompanied her visual inspection. "I've never shot a gun before." Her gaze locked onto his. "I'm not at all sure I can."

A self-deprecating smile stole across his lips. "You'll do what you have to when the need arises." He had little doubt in that department.

"Shouldn't he be here by now?" she asked, shifting her gaze to the house they'd come here to watch.

"Soon." The EMT's shift at the soup kitchen had ended twenty minutes ago. Cole suspected his arrival was imminent.

"How can you be sure this man—" She stopped and turned back to Cole. "Do you know our target's name?"

Cole didn't see the harm in sharing that information. "The man who died yesterday was Anthony Rice. Our final target, the man who visited your home and who continues to call, is Wyman Clark."

"How do you know he's the final target? What if there are more?"

Clearly she hadn't thought of that until now. "There could be others working for him but he's in charge." Clark was Cole's final target. He was the last of the original team involved with…the murder of Cole's brother and his family. When Clark was dead he would be finished. "If we take him down, the entire organization will collapse."

"There's an organization?"

"In a manner of speaking," he allowed. The details were of no consequence—a waste of time to discuss. An explanation would only lead her back to the question he had no intention of answering.

"But how can you be sure Clark hasn't already tracked down the EMT? Maybe he went to the soup kitchen."

"Miss Parker," he used her surname in an effort to keep things on a formal level, "I didn't allow him that opportunity. By the time Clark tracked down and interviewed the first EMT who was on duty, which would be the first, most logical place for Clark to start looking, the other man would be leaving his volunteer work at the soup kitchen." Cole glanced at the digital clock. "He should arrive home any minute now." He placed a tiny wireless communications device in his right ear to ensure his uninterrupted surveillance when the need arose for him to exit the vehicle.

Angel's prolonged silence made him uneasy. She was smart. He didn't need her figuring out the things she wouldn't understand.

"Oh my God."

Too late.

"You planned all of this, didn't you?"

A hint of terror tinged the words uttered with a kind of disappointed disbelief.

"Now is not the time to discuss strategy," he said, infusing his tone with a cold, calculating brutality. He trained his gaze back on the house.

"The guy who died didn't tell you anything, you only want Clark to think that. All of this…every moment was choreographed by *you*."

Any sign of fear, disbelief or disappointment had vanished, only unadulterated fury remained.

"Keep your voice down."

"To hell with you," she snapped. "What are you going to do? Let Clark go in there and hurt this guy for information he doesn't even have?"

Any response he gave at this point would be unacceptable.

He did the only thing he could…the only thing that would settle the matter once and for all.

The barrel of his weapon came to rest against her forehead before she could launch her next tirade.

"Shut your mouth," he warned, wiping any emotion, real or imagined from his mind. "Don't say another word. I won't let anything get in my way."

Her fingers tightened around the weapon in her lap but he knew she wouldn't use it. She lacked the essential ingredient—a heart of stone. Unless provoked by what she presumed to be the true enemy she wouldn't pull the trigger. Even then he wasn't so sure she would overcome the deeply engrained instinct.

At that precise second he discovered an unexpected glitch in his perfect plan. A rip in his longstanding impervious armor. In light of what he recognized just then, he had to admit that maybe it would have been better if she had used the weapon. Anything would be preferable to what he saw in her eyes and the power that discovery wielded. The glow from the moon provided ample illumination for him to see her initial shock fade to a combination of extreme disgust and dislike.

Headlights in the distance shattered the tension-filled moment.

Cole turned his attention back to where it belonged. He clenched his jaw against the alien emotions that tightened in his chest. What she thought of him was of no consequence. It would be best for all involved if she hated him, which he imagined would be the final outcome of their association…assuming either of them survived the night.

The compact car advancing toward their position slowed for the turn into the driveway. Cole visually identified the make of the vehicle beneath the beam of the streetlight as it swung into the drive. The EMT.

Clark wouldn't be far behind.

Cole's anticipation moved to the next level.

Time to finish this.

Lights came on inside the EMT's house.

Angel's impulsive move was abrupt and swift, but not swift enough. Cole snagged the arm closest to him before she had managed to open her door.

"Let me go!"

"Don't move," he ordered softly. "Clark will be close."

"You going to shoot me?" She peered up at him in abject disdain. "Well, go ahead."

He moved his head slowly from side to side. "You don't want to force my hand, Miss Parker."

"I don't believe you'll do it."

With one flick of his thumb he disengaged the safety of the weapon. "Are you sure about that?"

For two excruciatingly long beats he thought he had her, but then she proved him wrong.

"Yes."

She jerked out of his hold. The door opened and she was out of the car in one fluid move.

"I'm not going to sit here and let this man die for you."

He'd set the interior lamps to off, but even in the near darkness her determination was crystal clear.

"Not even for your aunt?"

She shut the door without answering.

Cole swore as she hurried across the street.

He had no choice but to watch for Clark. He couldn't make a mistake…not even to protect her.

No matter how badly he wanted to.

Angel pounded on the front door until the EMT opened it. He looked startled to have someone at his door this time of night.

"I'm sorry to bother you," she said quickly, scared to death Clark would arrive before she got inside. If he did, she was likely dead…unless Danes intervened and she wasn't sure he would—not if it put his mission at risk.

"I remember you," the big, burly EMT said. For the life of her she couldn't remember his name. "You're the lady from the shoot-out." He frowned, peered past her shoulder, his posture going from confident to nervous. "Where's that guy who was with you?"

"Can I come in?" She had to get inside. Lock the door. Now! "Please," she urged when he didn't look compelled to offer the invitation.

He shrugged. "I guess so. What's this about?"

He closed the door behind her. "Do you mind locking it?" She could only imagine how that request struck him.

"Look, lady, I don't know what's going on with you, but I'm beat." He hitched his thumb over his shoulder. "I got the shower warming up. Whatever you and your friend are involved in, I don't want any part of it."

She heard the water running somewhere down the hall. He just wanted to be left alone. Boy, did she know how that felt. But it was too late, he was in this.

"I don't know how to explain." She hugged her arms around her middle. She'd tucked her gun into the waistband of her jeans at the small of her back. She hoped she wouldn't need it. "Anything I say is likely going to sound crazy, but you're going to have to trust me."

He lifted a skeptical eyebrow. "Lady, after what I saw your friend do, nothing would surprise me."

She moistened her lips and tried to smile, it didn't work. Her lips just wouldn't make the transition. "The man who was shooting at us—the one who got away," she explained, "is coming. Here."

His uneasiness hitched up a notch. "Why? What does he want?"

How would she ever control this guy if he didn't believe her? He was far bigger than her. No way could she strong-arm him.

"He wants to know what his friend said before he died."

The EMT choked out a laugh. "Well that's easy. He didn't say anything. His voice was all garbled."

She nodded. "I know, but you have to understand, the man coming doesn't know. He believes his friend said something that you can tell him."

The EMT held up both hands stop-sign fashion. "Lady, I'm calling the cops."

What should she do now?

"You know—" she followed him into the kitchen where his phone hung on the wall "—under normal circumstances I'd say that's a good idea. But, I'm afraid that won't help."

He hesitated, his hand halfway to the receiver. Just then, for some reason she probably would never understand, the whole scene hit her from a new perspective. Here she stood, in this man's kitchen, trying to make him believe a story no one in their right mind would believe. He was just a regular guy with a job that put him in contact with lowlifes from time to time. He lived alone it appeared. His house was cozy, decorated in an old-fashioned way, as if maybe he'd inherited the place from his grandmother. And he had no idea that in the next few minutes he could die...probably would.

"You tell me what the hell's going on here." He advanced on her.

Angel held her ground, hard as that proved. "This man is a killer. He wants anyone involved with the shooting dead," she told him, giving him the abbreviated version.

"Then we need the police," he urged, desperation rising in his voice.

"No," she said softly. *If only it were that simple.* "What we need is a miracle." She thought of Danes. Tears burned in her eyes, but she blinked them away, leveled her gaze on the man standing before her in hopes he would see the desperation in hers. "But lately I've been having a little trouble believing in miracles. So, I think maybe it would be best if we got out of here."

His mouth opened but before he could speak a heavy knock rattled the front door.

She pressed her finger to her lips.

The terror that shot through her was reflected in the EMT's expression.

She grabbed him by the arm and moved silently into the hallway that adjoined the kitchen as well as the living room. The short corridor was dark but she followed the sound of the running water. A dim glow lit the small bathroom. Inside she closed the door and tried to lock it but the latch didn't work.

"It's broken," the EMT muttered.

Another pound on the front door.

"Look." She faced him. "He knows you're in here. Your car is in the drive and the lights are on."

"We shoulda called the cops," he whispered frantically.

A loud bang and the splintering of wood warned that Clark was coming in.

The EMT muttered a curse.

"Get in the shower." She shoved him toward the curtained tub.

"What?" he gasped.

"Get in. Hurry," she whispered.

He climbed into the tub. She climbed in right behind him and slowly pulled the curtain closed, painstakingly slowly so the metal rings glided across the chrome rod without making a sound.

She reached back and drew her weapon.

She spread her feet apart as best she could and held the weapon just the way the guy at the pawnshop had shown her. Hot water sprayed down on her but she ignored it. The EMT had moved to the far end of the tub, had pressed into the corner as far as he could. That was good.

She listened intently, trying to hear above the hiss of the water. If he opened the bathroom door did she fire then or wait until he drew back the curtain?

God, she didn't know.

Her heart surged into her throat. *Wait till he's close.* The pawnshop owner's advice rang in her ears.

She squeezed her eyes shut and did the only thing she could. She prayed for a miracle she feared would not come.

COLE WAITED UNTIL Clark entered the house before he moved. He moved in a dead run toward the vehicle Clark had driven. He hit the ground, ignoring the stabbing pain in his side. In less than ten seconds he had both tracking devices in place, along with a jambuster. A man like Clark would definitely have one or more jammers on board to prevent anyone from tracking his location. But Cole owned the latest technology in rendering those annoying devices useless.

He rolled away from the vehicle, gritting his teeth against the pain. He moved into the shadow of the trees at the side of the house and pulled out his cell phone. If this didn't work he'd have no choice but to go in. If he went in Clark wouldn't go down without a bullet between his eyes so that had to be a last resort.

He had to make this work.

He depressed the necessary function key and waited for the ring. He slowed his respiration, calmed his racing pulse.

Clark answered on the second ring.

"What the hell is it?" he growled, evidently believing the call came from one of his cronies.

"I'm waiting for you, Clark. Why don't you come and get me. Finishing this will be rather boring without your participation."

He ended the call.

Then he held his breath and waited for his target to take the bait.

ANGEL INCLINED HER HEAD, strained to hear.

A cell phone had rung. She recognized the sound.

She'd heard Clark's voice, recognized it, also, but couldn't make out his words.

He swore now, hotly, repeatedly.

That she comprehended perfectly.

Then nothing.

She held her breath…waited…listened.

Nothing.

Where the hell was he? Her pulse skittered into overdrive. Did she dare move?

The metal on metal grind of the doorknob turning split the air…cut right through the hiss of spraying water.

She heard the EMT's harsh intake of breath at the same instant that everything lapsed into slow motion.

Her grip tightened on the gun. She stared straight down the barrel and waited for the curtain to move.

The door creaked as it opened. Vaguely she noted that she hadn't noticed that before.

The distinct footfall on the floor. The whirr of metal gliding over metal.

Her finger twitched.

Her gaze collided with…

"Oh my God!" Her weapon clattered to the floor. "I almost shot you."

Danes lowered his weapon, glanced from her to the EMT and back. "We have to go. Now."

He assisted her out of the tub. "Stay someplace else for a couple of nights," he said to the EMT.

Angel glanced back at the poor guy. He'd huddled in the corner of the tub, his eyes wide. "Do you think he's okay?" she murmured shakily.

"He'll live."

Danes dragged her out the back door of the house and to the rented car.

"Where did Clark go?" she asked, suddenly realizing that she hadn't encountered his body. After the initial shock of seeing Danes on the other side of that shower curtain, she'd assumed he'd had to kill Clark.

"He's en route to your aunt's location."

Danes pushed her into the passenger seat. "What?" She couldn't have heard right.

He rounded the hood and slid behind the steering wheel before he answered. "He thinks we're there already." He started the engine and roared away from the curb, then tapped a keypad on what looked like a small, handheld computer. "We're tracking him."

Angel stared at the red dot moving on the map displayed on the screen. "Where is he now?"

"North on Highway 1."

She frowned, looked from him to the little computer and back. "How do you know that? You're not even looking at the screen."

He tapped his ear. "The route is being transmitted into my earpiece."

Mystified, she reached out and touched his hair. She should have known better, but she'd only wanted to pull it back and see the earpiece of which he spoke. He flinched. She drew back her hand in response.

He didn't want her to touch him.

Too bad.

Firming her resolve, she tucked his hair back so that she could see the tiny earpiece as they passed a street lamp. Wireless, she realized. She was aware that such technology existed.

"Neat." The single word sound stilted, but it was the best she could manage since the rest of her senses had zeroed in on the silky feel of his hair, the warm, smooth texture of his skin where she'd accidentally touched his jaw when she drew away.

She folded her hands in her lap, only then remembering that she'd dropped her gun in the EMT's bathroom. She stared down at herself and laughed tightly. She was soaked. The shower. God, she'd completely forgotten.

There was something else she'd forgotten. She turned toward Danes and said a silent thanks to God for sending her that miracle in spite of her lack of faith.

Chapter Eleven

The Port of Chicago, Midnight
10 hours, 15 minutes remaining...

Cole eased into an alley between two storage warehouses. The location made perfect sense. Clark and his men would have easy and immediate access to water or air transportation. A speedboat could be docked nearby for swift movement from the inland river system to the Great Lakes. A helicopter could be standing by on any number of helipads in the vicinity of the port. Every possible amenity had been added in recent years to lure in big business. Chicago liked being known as the "hub" of America's crossroads.

Operating 24/7, midnight comings and goings would not be considered suspicious. The sheer size and number of warehouses and facilities made the location a formidable maze, inadvertently, or perhaps not, allowing for a certain level of cover and anonymity. Getting lost amid the endless possibilities would be effortless for a man like Clark.

Were it not for Cole's state-of-the-art tracking devices and frequency bender that is. An antijam device, the bender, reconstructed twisted and broken frequencies, allowing the tracking devices to do their job.

He knew exactly where Clark was.

The warehouse looming to the left served as a temporary storage facility, square footage for lease to the highest bidder. Stephens had no doubt claimed a section or perhaps the entire building for his base of operations. Or maybe Leberman had held the lease for all these years, under an alias of course, to carry out his sinister plans.

"What now?"

The tremble in Angel's voice tugged Cole from his study of the structure and those inside. She shivered uncontrollably. He frowned. The heat was off now that they were parked allowing the cold night air to invade the interior of the vehicle. But not so much as yet.

Her clothes were wet.

The shower.

He swore softly, cursing himself for forgetting all else but the chase. He shouldered out of his jacket, gritting his teeth against the nagging pain involved. "You have to get out of those wet clothes." He couldn't believe she'd sat there the entire trip across town and said nothing about being wet and cold.

"I don't think so," she fired back.

"You can put this on." He offered his jacket. The thick lining of the leather jacket would provide adequate protection. The length would likely hit mid-thigh on her considering her much shorter stature.

Still she hesitated.

"You're a nurse," he reminded, "you know what it takes to bring the body temperature back up."

She snatched the jacket from him. "Turn your head."

"Don't worry, I'm going in. You get those wet clothes off and stay put."

"No way." She seized his arm. "You're not going in without me."

He'd anticipated this reaction and still the ferocity of her determination surprised him. Considering her damp clothes and the idea that she was freezing, he would have thought getting out in the night air would be the last thing she wanted. Obviously, he had underestimated her true grit.

"Yes. I am going inside alone. No arguments."

"Fine." She folded her arms over her soggy chest. "I'll just follow you."

She would. Even if he locked her in the truck she'd likely kick and scream, leaving him no choice but to set her free.

"Clark will have others in there. The shoot-out you witnessed this morning was nothing compared to how this might end." There was no point in lying to her. She needed to understand what they were likely walking into.

"My aunt is in there, right?"

He bit back his fury, not wanting to waste the energy. Exhaustion clawed at him. The pain, it was steady.

"Yes. I would assume she is here, but I can't be certain." If she was in there and she'd been killed already, he didn't need a hysterical woman on his hands.

"Then I'm going in. Turn your head." She peeled off her sweater to leave no question as to her intent. He looked away, but he couldn't block the sounds. Wet denim dragging over slim feminine hips, down-soft skin. The drop of a damp bra against the carpeted floor. The whisper of his jacket's lining as she pulled it on, the rasp of the zipper as she closed the leather around her.

He closed his eyes and inhaled a deep, cleansing breath. He needed to clear his mind of all the static associated with this thing between them. And there was a thing. An attraction of sorts. Something else he'd never permitted to happen while on assignment.

He was slipping.

"I'm ready."

Indeed.

The real question remained. Was he?

Pushing all other thought aside, Cole emerged from the car, motioned for her to slide out on his side. He reached into the back and retrieved his bag of tricks, then closed the door as noiselessly as possible.

Clark had parked his vehicle in the next alley. The entrance he'd used for accessing the warehouse would be nearby. He wouldn't leave much distance between himself and his escape route.

With his scanner in hand, Cole pressed against the brick wall as he moved in that direction. The scanner would alert him to any electronic surveillance in time to avoid its net. Angel shadowed his every step and move. She listened well when she wanted to.

For the moment he was glad she hadn't thought to ask how he'd gotten Clark out of the house back there. She wouldn't be pleased when she learned he'd had the capability of contacting Clark since he'd disassembled her cell phone and installed a descrambling device. The number Clark used on the next call had been obtainable.

She didn't have the proper experience to draw upon to enable her to understand how a man like Clark worked. He had to believe he was in control until the end. It was the only way to keep him on track. If he'd gotten spooked he would have changed his method of operation, made some unexpected move. Cole needed him to react based on a well-planned strategy, not his equally well-honed instincts. Clark would merely have killed Mildred Parker and disappeared until he regained the edge he'd had coming into this situation.

Patience was the only way to corner this kind of prey.

But Angel would never understand that.

She hadn't played this game. Cole had laid a trap and he'd waited.

In this game, the player with the most patience always, always won. No amount of strategizing or skill could outmaneuver a man with unending patience.

The element of surprise belonged to Cole.

The warehouse stood two stories and covered a sizable distance, perhaps a city block. The maze of alleyways and streets that surrounded the warehouses were lined with street lamps. The cover of darkness always worked as an ally. But not tonight. Tonight it was lacking.

He paused at the corner to the alley where Clark had left his four-door sedan.

Cautiously, he edged the scanner around the corner. It surprised him that no exterior electronic surveillance appeared to be in place. Whatever security Clark had in place, it would be inside.

Going in with Angel in tow would be risky at best. He turned to her and attempted once more to dissuade her from continuing.

"I need to go in alone," he told her bluntly. "There is no exterior surveillance which means it will all be inside. Moving around will be difficult."

"Forget it," she said in no uncertain terms. "I'm going in with or without you."

Cole braced against the rough brick wall, closed his eyes and fought a wave of vertigo. He couldn't waste energy arguing with her.

"I can't guarantee I can protect you in there," he said at last, admitting to his physical weakness. Another first. Bully for him. He felt like an alcoholic on the bottom three treads of the twelve-step plan. Going up was sure to be agonizing but going back down was out of the question.

"How bad is it?"

Well, now he hadn't expected that question. He opened his eyes and peered down at her. He'd anticipated her protests, even her denial that she needed his protection, but not this too knowing question.

"Not good."

She moved closer, searched his face. "The pain?"

He smiled but there was no humor in the gesture. "Nothing so simple as that. The pain I can deal with."

Her hand went to his forehead in the universal temperature-taking touch. "You don't feel overly warm. Tell me how you feel."

He drew her hand away, as comforting as her touch proved. "There's no time for this. The answer is, I felt like hell, but that's beside the point."

She shook off his hand and unbuttoned his shirt. She leaned down close to inspect the bandage. "No seepage. That's good."

"I shouldn't have brought it up." He pushed her hands away and buttoned his shirt. "I simply wanted to give you fair warning. I'm not exactly on my best game."

She harrumphed, an entirely rude sound. "Could have fooled me."

Then she walked right past him and into the alley.

Cole quickly caught up to her and pulled her back behind him. He put his face in hers. "We do this my way," he cautioned.

She backed away, offering her hands in a show of surrender.

He glared at her a second more, no longer trusting her seemingly shrinking ways. She'd grown herself a backbone a little too quickly.

The entrance was a steel door with a camera for identifying visitors. That avenue was out.

Cole walked the length of the building along the alleyway. Windows high above the ground, second-floor level he estimated, appeared to be the best possibility, but those would likely be wired to an internal alarm.

A roof access would be preferable.

At the end of the building the alley intersected with another. A ladder-type fire escape scaled the rear of the building's facade.

Excellent.

Still no detectable surveillance.

The iron ladder leading to the second floor and roof took its toll, but he managed. Once on the roof he slowed a bit to catch his breath.

A series of exhaust fans rose from the tarmaclike flat roof. Two doors, one on each end, offered access to the upper level of the building. Another architectural feature captured his attention and he moved toward it.

In the center of the mammoth roof was an enormous skylight. He approached it warily, uncertain what view would be provided. He kept Angel behind him. Obviously she hadn't realized his destination or what the pyramidlike structure offered.

A wide-angle, unobstructed view inside.

He crouched near the skylight to study the layout. Angel moved down next to him. The second level spanned the entire perimeter of the building like a narrow mezzanine. A number of doors on that level indicated offices and/or maintenance rooms. The lower level amounted to mostly wide-open space stacked three and four high with massive wooden crates. A shipping or main office claimed a portion of the warehouse floor on the far right.

Angel's gasp let him know she'd spotted Clark.

Clark stood, his back turned to their position, apparently arguing with another man who stood only a few feet away. The man clearly cowing to his boss's rampage was armed. Another man guarded the entrance Clark had used. No other comrades were readily visible.

Three, not such bad odds.

Clark suddenly stepped to the left and a woman, seated in a chair, her hands bound in front of her, came into view.

"Aunt Mildred."

Cole reached for Angel, pulled her against his chest. "Be very quiet, very still."

She nodded.

Clark ranted a while longer then gestured wildly toward the office.

The other man, the one who'd received the brunt of Clark's rage, pulled Mildred Parker to her feet and ushered her into what looked to be an office.

Clark entered a series of numbers into his cell phone and started to pace.

"Oh my God," Angel murmured. "He's probably trying to call us. I don't even know where the cell phone is."

Cole knew where it was. In the car. Turned off. But he had no intention of telling her that.

Clark closed his phone and rammed it back into his pocket. He strode toward the office, his movements filled with rage.

"We're going in now," Cole told her.

She held on to his shirt, her eyes wide with fear and brimming with tears. "Do you think he's going to hurt her now? He knows we've tricked him somehow."

"He won't hurt her until he knows he has us where he wants us."

She shook her head. "You told me you couldn't guarantee that."

He took her by the shoulders and held her firmly

with his hands as well as his eyes. "I know how this man operates. I understand his methods. Trust me."

She nodded, swiped at her eyes. "Okay. What do we do first?"

He picked up the scanner and tucked it into his bag. "Let's see what kind of obstacle the door is going to present."

They moved quietly across the roof to the door at the front of the building. Cole hadn't had a clean view of what the second level had to offer on the back side. Better the known than the unknown. He checked the door and its locking mechanism for security devices.

Just as he'd thought. The door was tied into the building's security. Would have been truly stupid had it not been. He delved into his bag and placed the necessary electronic devices on the door, then picked the lock the old-fashioned way.

With that out of the way he slipped the pack onto his back, had to stifle a groan. The burn of the sutures as well as the soreness related to the cracked rib weren't easy to completely disregard. She noticed his discomfort.

"You're sure you're up to this?"

"I'm fine."

She didn't miss the edge to his voice but allowed it to pass without comment. "What are those?" She pointed to the devices he'd installed.

"This door has sensors here and here." He indicated the locking mechanism and the top of the door. "Deactivating the lock won't be a problem, probably won't even show up on the security's monitoring system. But when the door moves away from its frame a fault message will trip the alarm."

"These little black boxes prevent that from happening?"

"Yes. They put off a signal that overrides the current one and remains constant regardless of the door's position. There's just one drawback."

Her gaze latched on to his. "What's that?"

"They only work for five seconds once the door is opened. We have to hurry."

She thought about that a moment, then nodded. "Okay. Let's do it."

He had to take a moment of his own. She stood on that roof, shivering from the cold air no doubt flying under the jacket which, as he suspected, hit about midthigh. She wore nothing else that he could see, except her socks and sneakers. She looked incredibly young and far too vulnerable to be involved with the likes of him.

He shook off the distracting thoughts. No time to think about that right now. He palmed his weapon, braced himself for a fight and opened the door.

The door closed silently behind them. If any alarm had been tripped it made no sound.

He surveyed the dimly lit stairs, scanning for electronics now as well as thermal images. He had no desire to run headlong into any of Clark's friends.

The stairs led down to the mezzanine. Fortunately the landing at the bottom of the last tread was tucked into a corner alcove. He waited, listening for a minute. A radio or television broadcasted somewhere in the building. The echo testimony to the lousy acoustics.

Staying out of sight in the alcove, he put his face close to Angel's, ensuring there would be no mistake in his words or his expression. The next few minutes would be crucial to their survival, as well as Mildred Parker's.

"I'm going to make a call," he told her, bracing for her reaction in much the same way he'd braced for moving in. "I'll give Clark a time and place. No bargaining. Dawn in Lincoln Park. The same ultimatum he gave us."

"Won't he know you're here? Trace the call or something?" As calm as she wanted the whispered words to be, he read the rising hysteria in her eyes.

"He won't know. My cell phone is secure, untraceable. He will probably rant and rave the way he did before, maybe worse. We'll have to ignore that. Eventually he'll calm down. When his guard has dropped enough, I'll make my move."

She chewed on her lower lip, the lushness making him ache to taste it…to soothe it with his own.

Finally she nodded. "Okay. I guess that's the best option."

Cole was not accustomed to waiting for anyone else's authorization or approval. Another crack in his armor.

"Trust me."

She searched his eyes, hers calm now. "I do."

He nodded. "Good."

Between their hiding place in the alcove and the radio or television, he felt confident his voice would not be overheard by the one man near the side door. There was at least a hundred yards between their locations.

Clark answered on the first ring. "Where the hell are you, you son of a bitch?"

Cole indulged in a smile. "Dawn, Lincoln Park," he told him casually. "Bring Ms. Parker unharmed and we'll finish this."

"I don't know what you think you're doing, Danes," he warned, "but I don't take orders from you. We'll do this my way or not at all. The game is over. I'm in charge."

"Not anymore. Lincoln Park. Dawn. My final offer. If you're not there, then you'll be looking over your shoulder for the rest of your life because I won't stop until one of us is dead."

"You smart-aleck bastard," he snarled. "If you knew where I was as you suggested in our last conversation, you'd be here. You don't know a damn thing."

"Perhaps. Are you willing to take that chance?"

Cole ended the called. Double-checked that his ringer was set to silent vibrate.

"What did he say?"

Cole didn't have to bother with a response. Clark stormed out of the office, sending the door banging against the wall.

"Am I surrounded by imbeciles?" he shouted. "You couldn't trace that call? Unbelievable! I thought you said we had the latest technology? How can some guy who works for NSA sneak under our net?"

"His signal bounced all over the country. Hell, even to Canada. I couldn't have locked in on his position if you'd kept him online an hour," his minion argued, albeit humbly.

Clark moved in on him, stabbed him in the chest with his forefinger. "What I want to know is how the hell he got my number."

Cole felt Angel tense next to him.

"We meet at Lincoln Park at dawn," Clark continued. "Assemble the rest of the team. I want them on-site well before dawn."

"Yes, sir."

Clark shouted to the man at the door. "Get your ass outside and start walking the perimeter. We've got things under control in here."

"Yes, sir." The man entered a code and slipped out the door to do as he'd been ordered.

Clark stood in the middle of the vast warehouse a second longer.

Cole tensed, drew farther into the shadows. The man's instincts were very good. He still felt that something wasn't as it should be.

Foolishly ignoring the instinct that had likely kept him alive many times in the past, Clark flipped open his phone once more, stabbed the necessary numbers.

He waited for an answer, apparently through three or four rings, then he said, "I want to meet."

Cole's tension moved to a new level. Who the hell had he just called?

"No." Clark shook his head. "Four o'clock this morning. I'll give you the directions en route." He provided a general direction for the caller. "Come alone or she dies. Is that clear?"

Satisfied with the response, he ended the call.

Clark glanced around the warehouse once more then disappeared into the office.

Cole waited ten minutes before making a move. During that time he considered who Clark could have called. Cole knew with complete certainty that Clark was the last of the original team. That he had at his disposal another team of mercenaries was no surprise. But to have a contact, someone who would care one way or the other whether Mildred Parker lived or died, was another factor altogether.

He looked at his watch—12:45 a.m. Three hours and fifteen minutes until this unknown person arrived. As much as he wanted to kill Clark right now he had to wait.

He'd literally had the man in his sights during that last phone call. But his man had been in the office with Ms. Parker. If ambushed, Clark's men likely had orders to execute the hostage. SOP. Standard operating procedures for military and civilian operatives alike.

It was a risk he couldn't take…not with Angel right beside him. He couldn't do that to her.

Cole scrubbed a hand over his weary face. He'd waited so long to finish this. How could he let anything get in the way?

Fate had played a very bad joke on him, it seemed.

Whatever the case, he had no choice now.

And he definitely needed to know who Clark had contacted. It had to be someone with ties to the Colby Agency. As unlikely as that seemed considering Cole's thorough investigation, it was the only answer.

Come 4:00 a.m. he would know.

After ten minutes of no activity below, Cole decided to make his move to better cover. A place he could safely leave Angel when the time came.

He inched out of the alcove and surveyed the options to his right. The flat panel doors he presumed to be offices or smaller, private storage rooms. One door, about three doors down, was clearly marked maintenance. That would be the one least likely to be locked.

Angel moved up beside him and he gestured to the

door. "Stay low, move slowly and quietly, but wait for my signal."

She nodded but didn't meet his gaze.

There was no time to ask questions now. Besides, he had an idea what was on her mind.

He crept out of the alcove, then moved quickly, keeping low as he'd instructed Angel, until he reached the door. Hoping like hell he'd chosen well, he turned the knob. The door opened without resistance. He visually checked the area below, beyond the mezzanine's railing, then motioned for Angel to come.

She did just as he'd told her, moved quickly, without hesitation.

Cole didn't breathe easy until they were both securely ensconced in their new makeshift quarters. He'd stuck a small, wireless video-and-audio transmitter to the outside of the door near the knob to keep tabs on the goings-on below. He used his tools to lock the door from the inside. With the right tools and skills, keys weren't necessary.

After switching on a small flashlight to cut through the consuming darkness he quickly placed a series of six matchbox-size black boxes around the small maintenance closet. The room housed a basic cabinet with sink, another floor-to-ceiling cabinet marked Supplies, and a mop and bucket propped in the corner. The odor of cleaning products lingered in the air.

"What are those?"

"In the event," Cole explained as he made the last adjustment, "Clark decides to use a thermal scan to detect the presence of warm bodies in the warehouse, these devices will conceal our presence. They mask the actual temperature of the room, ensuring that it shows up at a temperature comparable to the other rooms around it."

"Oh."

He set the flashlight on the sink, directing its beam toward the supply cabinet, allowing for some illumination of the space without calling attention to the door and any light that might slip beneath it.

Her expression was closed, her lips drawn in a grim line. He wondered how long this eye of the storm would last. Not nearly long enough for his liking he felt certain.

Focusing on the other necessary tasks, he set his handheld monitor to the right frequency and adjusted the zoom of the lens on the electronic eye outside the door. He set the sound on the midrange since he wouldn't be able to adjust it until there was actual sound coming from the targeted area.

He placed the monitor next to the flashlight and relaxed against the opposite wall. Now all they had to do was wait for 4:00 a.m.

"When were you going to tell me?"

So it began.

He opened his eyes and looked at her. "Tell you

what?" he asked, keeping his voice low in hopes she would do the same.

"That you could call Clark. That you had his number when you lied to me and said his call was impossible to trace."

"I told you what you needed to know, nothing more."

Fury gleamed in her eyes, giving the pale blue color a kind of iridescent quality. She closed the distance between them in two deliberate steps.

"I was worried sick that he wouldn't contact me again. You let me believe that."

"But he did," Cole countered, seeing no point in this exchange. "Your aunt is safe. In a few hours she'll be free and Clark will be dead."

"Why wait?" she demanded in a harsh whisper. "Why not just move in now. You've had a number of opportunities to shoot him."

"And the guy in the office would have executed your aunt. Don't think I didn't consider it."

A fraction of her anger diminished. "That still doesn't explain why you lied to me."

Ah, the proverbial "you lied to me" routine. They weren't lovers, they weren't even friends. His own anger sparked. He'd gotten her here. Her aunt was still alive. How the hell could she question his methods at this point? "I kept certain things from you because you weren't ready to hear the whole truth," he fired back, sealing his fate in her eyes.

He manacled her hand a split second before her palm made contact with his jaw. "Get some rest. We only have a few hours."

"I hate you," she whispered fiercely. "You're no better than they are."

He released her, lacking the energy or inclination to refute her claim.

She backed away, stopping only when she encountered the wall opposite him.

She was right anyway.

He knew what he was.

A man who left heavy collateral damage in the wake of each assignment. A man whose face and name few ever forgot.

No matter what happened this morning, she would not forget.

If only he could…just for a moment.

Chapter Twelve

1:55 a.m.

Angel fought the exhaustion dragging at her. She'd spent the last hour thinking of her sweet baby and her aunt, reliving the happy times. Those days seemed so far away now. She desperately hoped their future together would not end tonight. Her aunt was still alive and safe for the moment. Emotions tore through her. She felt too many to label them all. Relief, profound relief. Some level of uncertainty still. The past forty or so hours had been like a nightmare or a bad movie about someone else's life.

How could she have gotten in this deep with madmen like Stephens and Leberman? Don't leave Clark out, she reminded sarcastically. Why did they keep coming back? Leberman, supposedly the leader, was dead. Stephens was dead. Why couldn't the last of his men just let this whole thing go? Because terrorists died for their causes. And these men were nothing more than terrorists.

The thought sickened her, but it was true. Relentless bastards who cared nothing for anyone who got in the way of their goal. How on earth had her quiet, ordinary life attracted the attention of such madmen? The Colby Agency. Her aunt's connection to the Colby Agency. In a moment of utter clarity, Angel realized that her family, as well as Victoria Colby-Camp's were victims of the same terrorist. It wasn't supposed to make sense, it was the idealism of a man both obsessed and insane. Leberman had started it, his men would finish it.

And somehow the conclusion had something to do with Cole Danes.

Her gaze drifted to the man. His eyes were closed. Like her, he leaned heavily against the wall. Fatigue lined his face, the one that had grown so familiar to her now. It didn't take any stretch of the imagination to know his injury added to the burden. The pain would nag at him still. She thought of the way he'd thrown his body over hers that morning, of how he'd come through again tonight and rescued her and the EMT by distracting Clark somehow. That part still wasn't clear, but whatever he'd done, it had worked. She shuddered when she considered that she'd almost shot him. Her finger had been so close to squeezing the trigger. The relief she'd felt at seeing his face when that shower curtain drew back was immeasurable... indescribable.

Each step he'd taken, every single move he'd

made had been toward one end. Accomplishing his mission.

He'd found her aunt.

Now stood prepared to try and free her.

"Why can't we call for help?" she asked, voicing the next question that entered her mind. She cringed at how loud her words sounded in the cramped room when she knew she'd barely spoken above a whisper.

His eyes opened, the blue so dark it looked black in the dim lighting. "Any outside interference would motivate an attempt to escape. Your aunt would be executed. That's the way these men work."

She shivered at his words as well as the deep, rich sound of his voice. She shook herself. From the moment they'd met a war had started inside her. Part of her repulsed by his cold, relentless attitude, another drawn to him like a moth to the flame. "How can you be sure? If you told someone where we were, how many men they had and what their positions in the building were, it might work."

His eyes closed once more. "Don't believe everything you see on television, Miss Parker."

Fury whipped through her, shoving aside her fatigue. She wasn't that stupid. She abhorred his insistence on calling her *Miss Parker.* "It makes sense," she hissed, careful to keep her voice low in spite of her anger. "Anything's better than just standing here waiting." Claustrophobia had started to unravel her nerves or maybe it was merely the sound of his voice or even his words. She should have left well enough alone. She'd spent the last hour distracting herself with thoughts of her daughter and a happier past. Staying lost in the past had helped keep her calm. But now, reality was crashing back down around her.

Her aunt was in this warehouse. Angel's heart wrenched. There were only three men holding her just now. Surely a man like Cole Danes could take down those three. She said as much, laying down a challenge his arrogance would never allow him to disregard.

His eyes opened, and that laserlike gaze nailed her to the wall. "Yes, I could end this now. Even at three to one, the odds are in my favor. I have the element of surprise and I'm not afraid to die. The two men working for Clark are young, not nearly as experienced as he. They have no desire to die just yet. Taking them out would be a simple matter. Clark, however, would react on a wealth of experience in kill or be killed. He would take out the hostage first, then protect himself. He's not afraid to die, either."

Danes wasn't afraid to die. That was true. Not for a second did she doubt it. He'd covered her, pushed her to safety then lunged right into the hail of gunfire in that motel parking lot. Her heartbeat quickened at the terrifying memory. It seemed like a lifetime ago now. How could it have been just this morning? Well, technically, yesterday morning now.

At any rate, he'd risked death to save her. He would do it soon to rescue her aunt. She didn't want him to die. No matter how ruthless he wanted her to think he was, somewhere behind that relentless armor was a man who cared more than he wanted the world to know.

"Will waiting make this easier for you? I mean, help you do what you have to do?" She cursed herself for letting him hear her worry. Why couldn't she stay angry at him? She hated him.

That was a lie.

She didn't hate him at all.

She hated what he did. But she didn't hate him.

"The meeting at Lincoln Park is a diversion. I want them focused on something besides the here and now. Their distraction is essential to our success. But that's not why I'm waiting."

He intended to tell her. Her senses rushed to full attention. Did he finally trust her? Believe she could comprehend his ultimate plan?

"I'm waiting until Clark's 4:00 a.m. meeting," Danes went on. "He called someone and demanded a meeting. Someone who would care whether or not your aunt lived or died. I need to know who that someone is before I proceed."

She vaguely remembered the call. Somehow she'd missed a crucial element of the conversation. Obviously. If Danes were right, whoever Clark had called had some connection to her aunt.

The four o'clock appointment's identity would be important. For a number of reasons. Mainly to ensure that this was truly over. She wanted every connection to Leberman and Stephens exposed and squashed today. Her family would never be safe otherwise.

A weary sigh heaved past her lips. She should have trusted Danes to know what to do. Should have given him the benefit of the doubt. No matter how unconventional his means in her eyes, she should have trusted him from the moment he saved her life.

"Look." She hugged her arms around her middle and stepped toward him. "I owe you an apology," she said quietly. "I didn't mean to go off on you a little while ago." She stopped directly in front of him and met his wary gaze. "I don't hate you. I'm sorry I said that."

For several seconds she felt certain he wouldn't respond. He seemed to weigh his words as he searched her expression for some hidden motivation for the sudden about-face. She wasn't the only one around here who had difficulty with trust issues. Cole Danes had issues…lots of them. It didn't take a degree in psychology to recognize a man with a seriously screwed-up history.

"Don't give me too much credit, Miss Parker," he countered. "I'm not nearly as heroic as you believe. Saving your life was necessary to my endeavor."

She tamped down the automatic surge of anger at

his indifferent attitude. He had an explanation for every damn thing. Nothing was left to chance, nothing motivated by mere emotion. His every move, every thought was a carefully calculated strategy.

A new and startling epiphany abruptly intruded. That was exactly what he wanted her to believe. It kept her, like all other humans, at a distance. The question she'd asked earlier tonight surfaced amid the other chaos in her mind. Within the answer lay the truth about the real Cole Danes. She felt more certain of that conclusion than ever.

"Tell me," she challenged, determined not to be put off, "what did these men do to you? Somehow you got here the same way I did. *By personal express.* I know it. Don't try to deny it, *Mr. Danes.*"

He moved far too quickly for her brain to absorb his intent. His fingers plunged into her hair and hauled her face up to his. "Enough talk," he whispered against her lips. She gasped; he kissed her hard, punishingly so, smothering the tiny sound before it escaped.

She flattened her palms against his chest to push away, she told herself, but her strength melted in a flash fire of heat as her entire body zeroed in on his kiss. She wilted into his arms, unable to resist.

His lips felt firm and yet soft somehow. Hot, urgent. His body was hard beneath her palms. His arms a powerful bond around her, holding her close... closer.

His kiss was uninvasive, involving only his lips. But that was more than enough. Shiver after shiver skittered over her skin, penetrating more deeply with each caress of his mouth. Then he touched her lower lip with his tongue, swept from side to side, tracing the seam that instantly parted for him. He thrust inside. An *mmm* resounded deep in her throat. He tasted vaguely of the spicy sauce they'd shared from their drive-thru meal earlier. But the physical passion he exuded overwhelmed all other thought. Made her squirm to get closer to him.

His fingers traced her face tenderly, thoroughly, as if he wanted to memorize every minute detail. He drew back just far enough to look into her eyes, the feel of his ragged breath fanning her trembling lips. "You are so beautiful," he murmured softly before nipping her lower lip with his teeth. "Far too sweet and innocent for a man like me."

She felt his withdrawal even before his hands set her away from him.

Fury erupted inside her again, but it did little to quell the riot of desire. Damn him. He was the master of distraction. He'd wanted her to stop talking. Well, he'd succeeded. Only this time he'd made a strategic error in judgment.

She moved in on him, closer than before. "You're not getting off that easy." She grabbed his face and pulled his mouth back to hers. This time she launched the attack, kissing him with all the emotion that had been building since they'd first met. With all the need exploding inside her. She needed him. He would not deny her. Her fingers threaded into his silky hair. Damn, she did love his hair.

His hands were suddenly under the jacket, latching on to her bottom. He pulled her hips against his. She moaned at the feel of his craving for her. He was rock hard. Want slid through her veins, fueling the flames already out of control inside her. She hadn't been held like this in so long…hadn't felt a man's hungry touch…tasted a greedy kiss in so, so long.

She needed this…needed him.

The zipper of her jacket lowered. Strong fingers closed around her breasts sending more delicious shivers over her skin. She wanted him to feel the same. Slowly, her lips never leaving his, she unbuttoned his shirt. Then she reached inside, reveled in the feel of his sculpted chest, taking care not to get too close to the bandage or the holstered weapon. She felt him tremble when her fingers encountered his flat, male nipples. She smiled against his lips. In a bold move of payback, he slid one hand into her panties. She tensed, her heart thundering with sudden trepidation, her entire body anticipating the streak of sensations that would follow.

He wrapped his free arm around her waist and leaned her back as he bent forward, at the same time as one long finger slid inside her quivering body. The position intensified the daring invasion. She gasped.

Tried to kiss him but he evaded her, content to stare into her eyes as he plundered her drenched sex. His thumb pressed a hot button she'd almost forgotten existed, tightening her feminine muscles and sending a spiral of mind-numbing sensation cascading outward from the pulsing center. Her breath came in shallow little puffs as he drew response after response from her in this same manner, using nothing more than his magic fingers.

She fought the drugging effects of need. The urgent drive toward that precious pinnacle. Told herself not to let him do this. She wanted more than this. She wanted all of him. She wanted him to feel the pleasure, to reach this amazing peak. Too late. Her body went rigid, arched like a bow in his arms. Sensation after sensation rippled through her. Her muscles contracted greedily. She shuddered then felt her body go completely liquid.

He straightened, sagged into the wall, bringing her against his chest. His arms tightened around her, kept her vertical. She felt his heart pounding. Felt the hardness of his own flesh. She couldn't think clearly, couldn't understand why he'd satisfied her and not himself. The way he held her now…as if she mattered.

It didn't make sense.

Then she knew.

Distraction.

He didn't want to answer her questions. Didn't

want her working herself into a frenzy with killers
only yards away. Didn't want her dwelling on all that
could happen in the next few hours.

So he'd done what he did best, distracted her.

She pulled away from him. Stared into those carefully shuttered eyes. Her body still throbbed with the
lingering pleasure of the best climax she'd ever had.
She ignored it. Summoned her determination, di-
verted the irritation building toward one goal: breaking him.

She backed away, until she bumped into the
counter where he'd left the flashlight. She reached
behind her, felt the cool counter, then the colder edge
of the stainless-steel sink, moved beyond it until her
fingers closed around the cylinder shape of the flashlight. She positioned the light on the edge of the
counter where it met the wall. The glow formed a
spotlight on her target who still leaned against the opposite wall. His black shirt gaped open, revealing
that awesome chest. Her fingers had pulled his long,
silky hair loose around his shoulders. He looked
sexy, rumpled and entirely dangerous since he still
wore his shoulder holster and gun. But she no longer
feared him. His posture stiffened as she watched.
Good. She wanted him on guard, wanted him to lose
his cool. Her gaze dropped to the black trousers he
wore. Some things just couldn't be hidden. That willing and ready hard-on definitely wouldn't be ignored. Not by her anyway.

A smug smile lifted the corners of her mouth. Maybe he was right, maybe she shouldn't believe everything she saw on television. But the one thing TV, movies and books alike had in common—at times like this the power of a determined woman could move mountains.

She hoisted herself up onto the counter, the chilly surface making her buttocks flinch. She opened the jacket wide and spread her legs in invitation. His intent gaze followed her every move.

She shouldered out of the jacket, let it fall onto the counter behind her. She watched that glittering gaze shift to her breasts. To further tempt him, she touched one taut peak. He'd made her that way. Had her breasts aching for more of his touch. His nostrils flared, his ragged breath audible in the otherwise silent room. She dropped her hand to her thigh, trailed her fingers toward the juncture there. Excitement rushed through her, settled in her sex. But it was his primal reaction that flooded her with the renewed heat of anticipation. He literally trembled. His jaw hardened. The effort to physically restrain the primitive need she had awakened undeniably visible.

Now for the final move to render him helpless, she mused. She waited for him to have his fill of staring at her body, then, when his gaze met hers, she laid down the true gauntlet. "I hope that wasn't the best you have to offer, *Mr. Danes.*"

He closed the distance between them in one fluid

stride. Cradled her face in his hands and issued an ultimatum of his own. "Just remember," he warned, his deep voice as lethal as the savage gleam in his eyes, "you asked for this."

His mouth claimed hers in an open kiss so brutal she whimpered. But the pleasure of his touch…of her victory far outweighed the minor discomfort. The oxygen evaporated in her lungs like rain falling on a hot rock. His kiss proved every bit as relentless as the man, his hot tongue as masterful and bold as the pirate she'd likened him to on first sight. The feel of his trousers rasped against her wanton flesh. The counter held her at the perfect height for direct contact. Her trembling hands went to his fly. She wanted him now, wanted to feel him in her hands.

He pulled back, pushed away her searching hands. "Don't move," he ordered, his tone nothing short of barbaric.

That relentless gaze held her utterly paralyzed. The only muscle in her body able to move was her heart, it floundered helplessly. Her entire soul stilled, anticipating his next move.

The hiss of metal gliding over metal accompanied the lowering of his fly. She wanted to look, couldn't move…couldn't take her eyes off his. Not even the blood roaring in her ears could drown out the sound of rustling fabric as he reached in and freed himself. A muscle in the granite of his jaw flexed. She dragged in a jagged breath, her lungs begging for air.

Felt the heat of his sex and he hadn't even touched her.

His fingers clutched her thighs and dragged her closer to the counter's edge. She rolled her pelvis in expectation, couldn't look away from those devastatingly intense eyes.

The first nudge made her gasp. Her eyes closed in ecstasy. His fingers threaded into her hair, cradled her head. "Look at me," he whispered, commanded.

Somehow she managed to open her eyes. Though she didn't know how. She couldn't think past the feel of him pressing into her. It had been so long since she'd felt this way, since she'd wanted anyone. And she'd never wanted anyone the way she wanted Cole Danes.

His fierce gaze holding her captive, he pushed beyond her opening, hesitated only a second. She cried out softly. Her body quivering, wanting. Then he thrust fully, didn't let up until he was deep inside her and even then he reached back with one hand and ushered her more firmly against him, completing the seal. The fingers of that same hand glided down her leg, lifted it around his waist.

"You feel that?" he whispered. "That's the *best* I have to offer."

She nodded. Her body throbbed, felt filled to capacity and then some. She trembled violently, but with pleasure not fear. Closed her eyes at the sheer sweetness of it. It felt so good.

He lowered his other hand, allowing her head to loll back as he trailed those long fingers along her other leg, lifted it, anchoring her completely around his waist.

The sensation of being filled, of stretching to accommodate his generous size, intensified.

"Look at me," he repeated.

Her lids fluttered open. Those dark eyes measured her expression, her reaction. The lines and angles of his face taut with restraint. That earring glinted in his ear reminding her again of a pirate on some ancient ship. He'd already rendered her utterly helpless. She could only wait for him to finish this. And here she thought she'd prove something. Not in this lifetime.

He took his time, flexed his hips maybe an inch, a slow in and out, just enough to shatter any semblance of control she grappled for.

"What do you want me to do, *Angel?*" One corner of that smug mouth lifted ever so slightly. "You wanted this, tell me what to do next."

Bastard. She tightened her legs around him, drawing him even deeper inside her. He didn't flinch, showed no outward reaction. "Don't pretend you don't feel this," she countered just as fiercely. "I know you do."

"You're wasting your time," he growled, putting his face closer to hers, teasing her lips with his own. "What do you want? Do you want me to make you come again? Just say it. Because that's all you're going to get from me."

She grabbed him by the shirt front and held on, determined not to let his uncaring words stop her. "Then shut up and do it."

Something changed in his eyes. A flash of surprise or maybe regret. He braced his hands on the counter and drew back, all the way to the tip, then drove into her with such force that she lost her breath. Again and again he withdrew, thrust deeply. She didn't want it to happen this way. Didn't want to let him do this…not like this. But she couldn't stop her body's plunge toward release once more.

Everything around her faded to insignificance. All his funny little electronic devices. The madmen below. The fear for her aunt's safety as well as her own. Nothing else mattered. She could only watch his unchanging face. Feel him sliding in and out of her. She wanted to resist…wanted to deny his power over her. But it was impossible.

She came. Forcefully. Couldn't hold out any longer, couldn't block the sensations.

His movements slowed.

She forced her eyes open. Saw the sweat on his forehead, the muscle pulsing rapidly in his jaw. Her hopes fell, her thrashing heart wrenched painfully.

But then she saw him tremble. Just a little.

She pulled his face near once more, kissed him

with all the desperation screaming inside her. "Don't you dare stop," she murmured.

He made a sound that ripped through her emotions. A guttural reverberation of helpless remorse, something intensely vulnerable. Something totally unDaneslike.

He thrust again. Shuddered visibly. She kept her arms around his neck, kept him close. Urged him on. He pumped in and out, his movements growing frantic. Not like before. Not controlled. Not brutal. Frantic and desperate. Needy.

Incredibly her utterly sated body reacted. Started to rush toward that peak of pure sensation all over again.

He didn't give in easily. He waited for her to catch up. Climaxes erupted simultaneously. This time it wiped her out. Every ounce of energy and emotion she possessed seeped from her as if she'd died in that final moment.

But she wasn't dead.

And neither was he.

He sagged against her. His weight making her tremble with relief. Making the tears stinging her eyes flow down her cheeks.

She'd conquered him for just that one moment.

Seen his vulnerability.

And like the man, it was overpowering—shook her as nothing else ever had.

Then she realized her mistake.

With his vulnerability had come her own. She'd let down all her defenses in an effort to break his, had sacrificed herself to reach him.

She'd fallen for him—fallen in love with a man incapable of loving her back.

Chapter Thirteen

Cole pulled out and quickly righted his trousers.

What the hell had he done?

He reached for the roll of paper hand towels mounted above the sink, pulled off a few and offered them to her. "Clean yourself up."

When she'd scooted off the counter he washed his hands and turned his back to give her some privacy.

How could he have been so stupid?

He'd been slowly losing it since laying eyes on her and now... Well, now he'd really screwed up.

He never made mistakes like this.

But she'd pushed him.

He closed his eyes and swore softly.

She'd pushed him until he couldn't do otherwise.

Yet, he couldn't blame her. He'd started it with that kiss. He'd made a mistake.

No condom. Nothing.

Stupid. Stupid!

Not that he feared disease from her. She didn't

fool around—hadn't, as best he could ascertain, since the man who'd fathered her child. Pregnant women were tested for most anything a sexual partner would need to be concerned about.

"I don't usually have unprotected sex," he told her, in case she might be wondering the same thing. "You don't have to worry about that."

The water running in the sink was his only response.

"That shouldn't have happened," he added, more to himself than to her.

"Why?"

He faced her, saw the anger in her pale eyes.

"Because it proves you're human?" she tossed in for good measure.

Why lie? "Yes."

She'd zipped up the jacket, hiding the gorgeous body she'd so readily displayed minutes ago. She was so beautiful. His muscles contracted with want. The insistent ache in his side reminded him that he'd been shot recently. But he didn't care. He only cared that her sweet face showed signs of his aggression. There would likely be bruises on her arms tomorrow where he'd held her too tightly. There would be other aches, as well. He'd given her what she wanted, savagely so. All in an attempt to walk away unscathed.

It hadn't worked.

But she didn't have to know that.

She came toward him, her tousled hair making

him want to touch it. His fingers itched to go there. Soft, like silk, like an angel's hair. He wondered if that's how she'd gotten the name. She looked like an angel. So pale and ethereal, like a vision. Her blue eyes so translucent they reminded him of light reflecting off water. All captured in a beautiful face that broke through his defenses with such ease.

"You still didn't answer my question." She lifted her chin in defiance of the emotions still glowing in her eyes. "What did Stephens and Leberman do to you?"

He took a moment to check the monitor. Nothing. Clark hadn't come out of the office, nor had the other man. The third man remained outside, likely freezing. Maybe he would freeze and that would be one less life to take to accomplish his mission.

"I won't stop asking until you tell me," she prodded. "You might as well get it over with."

He relaxed against the wall, took his time buttoning his shirt, then adjusted his shoulder holster. "What difference does it make?" A flagrant stall tactic.

She shrugged self-consciously. The answer would be more telling than she wanted but if she wanted him to spill his guts, then she would, as well.

"I want to understand you," she admitted. "I need to know what drives you. What makes you push the rest of the world away?"

This had gone too far already. He didn't like what

he saw in her eyes. He wasn't the right kind of man for her and he didn't want to hurt her. The father of her child had done that rather well four years ago.

His own questions nagged at him. Things he suddenly wanted to find out when he knew with complete certainty that this impulse was utter foolishness, supreme stupidity.

"All right. I'll answer your question if you answer mine."

"Mine first," she interjected. "You already know a lot more about me."

"Fair enough." He folded his arms across his chest, gritting his teeth against a particularly nasty jab of pain. Overly aggressive sex wasn't exactly a smart move under the circumstances, but a long-buried flaw in his personality wouldn't let him regret the actual act. It was the consequences that bothered him.

"Where do you want me to start?"

He should never have asked that question.

"Where were you born?"

He glanced at his watch. "We only have two hours," he reminded—and that was assuming Clark didn't make any unexpected moves.

She looked at him expectantly.

He exhaled a heavy breath. "I was born in Louisville, Kentucky."

"Really?" Her expression brightened at the prospect of learning his secrets. "You don't sound Southern."

He laughed faintly. "Kentucky may or may not make me Southern but that was a long time ago."

"So you grew up in a city?"

He shook his head. "On a horse farm. City folks like you would call it a ranch."

"Horses? You ride and everything?"

"I used to. I actually spent a number of years in South Africa. My father was an ambassador."

"Incredible."

He rolled his eyes feigning impatience. "It's not that incredible."

"Keep going," she prompted.

"My mother and father have since retired from politics as well as horses to a vacation home in Florida. The farm still operates, breeding horses and the like but they rarely get back there."

"And what about you, do you ever go back there?"

"No."

Angel sensed the change in him instantly. He didn't want to talk about his life. The extraneous was acceptable, but not his actual connection to any of it.

"Any brothers or sisters?"

"One brother. He's dead."

Something about the way he said the last made her apprehensive. She wasn't sure she should pursue that avenue just now. His expression had closed completely. Time to take a page from his book of lessons. Distraction.

"So where did you go to college?"

"Yale."

"Wow. Yale, that's…" A frown furrowed its way across her forehead. "You must be really smart."

The shadow of a smile dimpled one jaw. "Not so smart."

"What does a smart guy who goes to Yale major in?" Her distraction had apparently worked.

"Law, with an emphasis on foreign affairs."

"You could have become a politician or gone on to become a lawyer," she teased, knowing he definitely lacked the necessary bedside manner, so to speak, for either.

"NSA recruited me my final year in law school."

"NSA?"

"The National Security Agency. They were looking for graduates trained in foreign languages. That I spoke several flagged my file. My studies in foreign affairs only added to my value in their eyes."

"What does a multilingual lawyer do at NSA?" Moving into hazardous territory again, she realized as his posture stiffened.

"I'm afraid that's classified."

She nodded, not doubting it for a second. "What happened to your brother?" She almost cringed, had hoped to slide that one in but he was far too fast for her.

He stared at her for a second that turned to ten, his gaze looking right through her, lost in some time

and place in the past. When he finally spoke his
words were hollow.

"He was murdered."

She sucked in a sharp breath. "How?" She
hadn't meant to ask that. She should have left that
subject alone.

"He worked for the State Department. He and his
family went on a goodwill mission to Libya. The VIP
vehicle that picked them up at the airport exploded.
Everyone was killed."

He didn't have to say more. "Leberman and
Stephens were involved," she guessed.

"I didn't know until several years later. I used my
position at the NSA to do some investigating beyond where others had left off."

Her pulse accelerated at the horror he and his parents must have suffered. She wanted to reach out to
him but knew her comfort, any kind of comfort, was
unwanted.

"I'm sorry."

"So am I."

She stared at the floor unable to bring herself to
look at him. He wouldn't want her to see any emotions he might not be able to hide. She understood
that about him. He didn't like being vulnerable and
that obsession became suddenly, agonizing clear.
Being vulnerable had gotten his brother and his family killed. A man wouldn't find himself vulnerable
if he kept the world pushed away.

"My father hounded me to let it go," he went on to her surprise. "He, apparently, didn't want to risk losing another son."

"How are your parents now?" Time was the great healer but she doubted any amount of time would be nearly enough to heal that kind of wound.

"I have no idea. We don't talk at all."

Disbelief pushed past all other emotion. "Because you're obsessed with vengeance?"

"Yes," he said succinctly. "And I will finish it."

Angel pressed a tremulous hand to her mouth as she absorbed completely the full impact of what she'd learned. "That's why you're here." She breathed the words, a new kind of fear making her voice falter.

"It has taken me eight years, but they're all dead now except one. Clark. He will die this day."

"You killed them all?" He'd led a one-man hunt, played judge, jury and executioner.

"All but one. Leberman. Someone else took care of him."

As he'd told her this awful truth she'd watched the cold, hard mask he'd worn when she first met him fall into place. She'd been wrong about him being afraid to be vulnerable. That wasn't it at all. The real reason he kept everyone at arm's length, even his own parents, was so that he could be an unfeeling, relentless machine. He'd closed out the world.

He inclined his head and studied her in that arrogant way he had of lending intimidation. "Now you know."

She nodded. "Now I know."

Her gaze drifted down to her hands. She thought about the way his skin had felt beneath her touch, hot and smooth. The way he'd held her after the first time she'd come apart at his touch.

"Cole." She approached him, uncertain how he would respond. It was the first time she'd called him by his first name without taking it back. "You did what you had to. If someone had done this to me, I would have reacted just as you did. I actually tried. I even bought a gun. You're punishing yourself for doing the right thing. You can't let it keep eating at you."

His gaze collided with hers, the fury there making her take a step back. "It has a name. Vigilantism. I killed those men in cold blood. Don't forget I know the law. Murder one. So don't try to pretty this up. I know what I've done. I don't regret it."

"But you knew they wouldn't stop." She reached out to him, let her hand come to rest on his arm. That he didn't flinch or draw away gave her courage to continue. "You did what you had to. What no one else had been able to do."

That fierce gaze wavered just a little. "Don't do this. Don't even bother." He laughed but the sound held no malice. "Don't try to save me, Angel. I know what I am. What I've done."

She lifted her chin in defiance of his summation. "You're right. I don't have to try and save you. I

know you, better than you think. When you've finished this, you'll save yourself."

That's where the conversation ended.

He didn't even bother taking his turn.

She'd said more than enough for both of them.

The only thing they could do now was wait.

3:45 a.m.

COLE BENT OVER the handheld monitor watching the
activity below.

Rather than give his appointment a final destination Clark had ordered two members of his team
standing by at Lincoln Park to intercept his expected
guest en route to an unknown destination.

Clever.

Stephens had chosen wisely when he picked this
one. Too bad his time on this earth was sorely lim-
ited. Clark would be the next to die.

Angel whimpered in her sleep. Cole glanced in
her direction. She'd settled on the floor in the corner, her legs pulled tightly to her chest. He looked
away. Unable to bear the idea of her getting hurt in
the events about to take place. There was only one
way he could ensure her safety.

He'd searched the supply cabinets and found duct
tape. That should hold her.

He checked his weapons once more. The one in

his shoulder holster and the one at his ankle he'd retrieved from his pack. He was ready.

His gaze drifted back to Angel. She wouldn't go along with this. That left him with only one option.

He crossed the small room and crouched next to her. "Angel," he whispered. "Wake up. It's time."

Her lids fluttered opened, revealing those luminescent blue eyes. "What time is it?"

He pressed his finger to his lips. "Almost four."

He assisted her to her feet.

"What're they doing down there?" Her gaze moved to the monitor.

"Turn around," he ordered quietly.

Her gaze swung back to him. "What?"

He made a circular motion. "Turn around."

She looked at him. "What're you doing?"

"Making sure you stay safe."

When she would have argued, he plastered a piece of the two-inch-wide tape across her mouth. She glowered at him and reached for the offending tape.

He shook his head, touched the butt of his weapon in warning. Her eyes widened in surprise. He averted his, not wanting to see the hurt or disappointment that would surely be there, as well.

When he'd turned her around, he bound her wrists behind her, then ushered her back down to the floor. He wound a few loops of the tape around her ankles.

"I assume you know better than to make any

noise," he noted. "Giving away my presence wouldn't help your aunt."

He did look at her then. She looked ready to murder him. He almost smiled. Good girl. *Don't let a bastard like me get you down.*

He told himself it was a mistake but he just couldn't resist. He kissed her forehead and murmured, "Take care."

He didn't look back for fear of changing his mind. Instead he unlocked the door and slipped out, keeping a close eye on the monitor.

Before dawn it would all be over.

LUCAS CAMP HAD NO CHOICE but to allow the two men to escort him inside the warehouse. He'd kept the appointment just as the man who'd called had requested. Lucas had insisted his team of Specialists stay as far back as possible. Risking Mildred's life was a chance he wasn't willing to take, not even to safeguard his own. His men wouldn't be far behind. Still, as he walked toward where a man waited in the middle of the main warehouse floor, he couldn't help feeling uneasy. He was unarmed and a pair of police-issue handcuffs rendered him pretty much powerless.

"The master spy, Lucas Camp. Well, well, we finally meet."

Lucas waved off his inspired greeting. "I'm afraid you have me at a distinct disadvantage."

"Ah," the man said in mock surprise. He extended his hand. "Wyman Clark."

Lucas declined the gesture. "One of Leberman's recruits," he suggested.

"I was recruited by Howard Stephens actually."

"Do tell," Lucas said facetiously. "And to what do I owe the distinct dishonor of this clandestine rendezvous?"

Clark gestured for three of the four men present to go outside. He no doubt suspected that Lucas would have backup.

"I'm afraid you've caused me quite an inconvenience," Clark said then. He nodded to the fourth man present and he retreated to what looked like an office only ten or so yards behind his boss.

"I'm certain it wasn't inconvenience enough since you're still breathing," Lucas returned, seeing no point in keeping up the ridiculous chatter.

A red fury rimmed Clark's thick neck. "Cole Danes has proven a far worthier opponent than we anticipated. Since you commissioned his assignment to find and destroy me and the only remaining original member of my team, I thought you might like the pleasure of watching him die."

"Unfortunately," Lucas told him, garnering a great deal of glee from revealing this little tidbit, "I can't take credit for siccing him on you and your team. He's been picking you off one by one for years."

Clark looked bewildered. "Impossible. Only one of my men was killed by professionals, the others had unfortunate accidents."

Lucas smiled knowingly. "Unfortunate accidents orchestrated by Danes. And now, you're the last man standing. Didn't your buddy Stephens tell you before he took that swan dive off that mountain? I'm sure he must have figured out the connection."

The red bloom of fury crept up Clark's neck and over his face. "No NSA paper pusher would be good enough to take out one of my men, much less three."

"I guess we'll just have to agree to disagree. Why don't you ask him for yourself? He's probably here right this minute, watching you."

Clark glanced around, a nervous sweat breaking on his forehead. "No more games," he snarled. "Maybe you're right, maybe he is here. That would be good. He can bear witness to what his elusiveness has caused."

The fourth man emerged from the office. Mildred, bound and gagged, struggled in his hold.

Lucas felt the air rush out of his lungs. He couldn't let Clark kill her. Her frantic gaze landed on Lucas's and she let out a moan that ripped him apart inside.

"Let her go, you son of a bitch. You have me now."

"What I have," Clark countered, "is a helicopter standing by. I know when I'm cornered. But you haven't seen the last of me." He glanced back at the man holding Mildred. "Kill her."

"You don't have to do this," Lucas urged, keeping the desperation he felt out of his voice. "Let her go. Take me."

Clark laughed. "Oh, no. It's far too much fun to watch you squirm knowing there's absolutely nothing you can do to save her."

Clark walked away, leaving his man with a gun to Mildred's temple.

Lucas readied to ram him. If he got off a shot Mildred would die, but, as it was, she was dead anyway.

A shot exploded in the air.

Lucas blinked.

The man holding Mildred dropped to the floor.

The side entrance flew open and another of Clark's men rushed in. Lucas rushed against Mildred, taking her down to the floor and shielding her body with his own.

More shots shattered the silence.

ANGEL'S MOVEMENTS became more frantic when she heard the shot. She didn't know what was happening out there but she had to do something.

She rubbed the tape binding her wrists against the corner of the countertop until she'd succeeded in tearing it. She quickly struggled out of it now. Ripped the tape off her mouth and then from her ankles, ignoring the sting.

The monitor was blank. Had he turned it off?

She didn't have time to figure it out. She resisted

the urge to run out the door. A weapon. She needed a weapon.

She dug through his backpack. Her fingers curled around a gun very much like the one she'd purchased. There was a clip in the handle and a similar safety mechanism.

She released the safety and pushed to her feet.

Okay. She could do this.

Angel moistened her lips and forced her respiration to slow, her heart to calm.

Focus. Pay attention to the details the moment you open the door. Don't waste any time.

She eased the door open and moved across the narrow landing to the railing. Below on the warehouse floor, a man lay atop her aunt in the middle of the floor. A scream rushed into Angel's throat but she swallowed it back.

Moving. Her aunt was moving. The man on top of her was checking her.

Safe.

She was safe.

Cole. Where was Cole?

Movement in her peripheral vision snagged her attention. Near the side entrance. Cole and another man rolled around on the floor. How could she help?

She stared at the gun in her hand, then at the men struggling. No way to shoot without maybe hitting Cole.

Another flurry of activity drew her gaze to the left.

She looked toward the far corner of the mezzanine just in time to see someone barreling up the stairs toward the roof.

She blinked.

Clark.

He was getting away.

She ran after him.

He couldn't get away.

It would never be over...

She thought of her baby girl.

Mildred was safe. She would take care of her baby.

She had to stop Clark—had to end this.

Dragging in a bolstering breath, she clenched her jaw and ran as fast as she could to the stairs. She didn't slow down to think...didn't lose her focus until she'd reached the very top.

Angel burst through the door and onto the roof. Wind whipped around her.

A helicopter sat near the skylight.

Clark ran toward it.

She took aim. Steadied her arms. Spread her feet apart.

Her left shoulder jerked.

She stared down at it. Saw the blood bubble through a strange hole in Cole's jacket.

The pilot in the helicopter had shot her.

She ignored the burn of pain.

Squeezed the trigger.

Glass exploded.

The man in the helicopter fell to one side.

She hadn't shot him?

Had she?

Clark suddenly turned. His weapon leveled in her direction.

She fired again.

He stumbled back, but didn't drop his weapon.

She fired again.

He fell back onto the asphalt roof. Was he dead? His arm moved.

She shot him again.

His body twitched.

She fired again.

"I think you can stop shooting now, ma'am."

Angel swung to face the voice.

A man dressed in combat gear held out his hands in a calming gesture. "Lower your weapon please."

She glanced back at Clark. "Has he stopped moving?" Tears were pouring down her cheeks. Her whole body trembled so violently she could hardly stand.

"Yes, ma'am, he won't be moving anymore."

She turned back to the man in black. "Who are you?"

"I'm Specialist John Logan. I'm here with Lucas Camp."

Her strength evaporated in a mist of exhaled tension. She dropped the gun. Fell to her knees.

It was over.

She'd killed him.

The man named John Logan helped her to her feet. "Let's go inside, ma'am. It's clear now."

Her gaze collided with his. "Clear, what does that mean?"

"It means the enemy has been neutralized."

"What about my aunt? Cole?"

"Your aunt is safe. One man inside is injured, one is dead."

God, don't let it be him.

John Logan helped her down the stairs since she felt too weak to walk on her own. The dizziness just wouldn't go away. Her vision faded in and out of focus. She knew the symptoms but she refused to faint just yet. She had to be sure.

When they reached the mezzanine she broke free from the man named Logan and ran to the railing. Her aunt sat in a chair, a man kneeled beside her, visually examining her. An EMT, maybe only he was dressed in black combat gear like Logan.

Where was Cole?

A motionless body lay on the floor near the door. Her heart stalled in her chest.

No. It wasn't Cole.

Thank God.

Then she saw him.

He stood a few yards away talking to Lucas Camp.

Relief rushed through her. She half stumbled down the remaining stairs that took her to the main warehouse floor.

She suddenly stopped, felt torn. She looked from her aunt to Cole and back. His gaze collided with hers across the distance. She pressed her hand to her mouth to hold back a sob. She wanted so badly to run to him.

"Angel!"

Her aunt's voice drew her in that direction.

She hugged the woman she loved with all her heart.

"Thank God you're safe," Mildred Parker murmured over and over as she hugged and kissed her niece.

Angel drew back and swiped at her eyes. "You're okay?"

Mildred made a scoffing sound. "They couldn't kill me," she protested. "I haven't lived this long without learning a few things." Her aunt winked at her and Angel knew then that everything would be all right. Despite the slightly shaken look in her eyes, she wore her usual unstoppable facade.

She kissed her aunt's cheek. "There's something I have to do."

"Go on. I'm fine." Mildred ushered her off so the man waiting nearby could continue his examination.

Angel hesitated for a moment thinking she should be doing that. She was a nurse.

"Go," Mildred urged, a knowing look in her eyes.

Angel nodded. She pushed to her feet, her legs still feeling shaky. A searing pain shot through her arm. She'd forgotten about getting shot. Wasn't it supposed to hurt worse than this?

Shock, she told herself. Shock was setting in.

She turned to go to Cole, but he was gone. She frowned, closed her eyes a second and then looked again.

He was gone.

"Ma'am, I need you to sit down and let me have a look at your shoulder."

She looked up to find the man named Logan standing next to her. "Where's Cole Danes?" she asked, almost startled by how strange her voice sounded. A sudden wave of wooziness washed over her.

"You need to sit down, ma'am."

"I'm…where's…"

And then the lights went out.

Chapter Fourteen

Inside the Colby Agency,
9:00 a.m...the morning after

"I can't believe it's really over." Victoria Colby-Camp looked to her husband for final confirmation.

"It's over," Lucas confirmed. He turned to Cole then. "I don't know whether to thank you or have you arrested," he said, annoyance muddying the relief he clearly felt. "You endangered both Mildred's and her niece's life. As well as your own," he added with a raised eyebrow. "Not to mention that of Jayne Stephens and Heath Murphy."

"I did what I was commissioned to do," Cole reminded him. That this assignment coincided with his own personal quest was purely accidental...or fate if one believed in such things.

"Mr. Danes." Victoria leaned forward, the leather of her luxurious executive chair crinkling with her movement. She settled her clasped hands on her polished mahogany desk. "There are no words to adequately convey my gratitude."

Well, that was a change. Most were too furious with him at the end of an assignment to admit he'd done what they'd asked him to do.

She blinked but not before he saw the emotion clouding her vision for that one instant. "You cannot know what Leberman has done to my family." She stared at her hands a moment. "You've read the accounts, of course." Her gaze returned to his. "But you can never really know."

But she was wrong.

"Leberman's legacy is finished," Cole stated with finality. He allowed her to see the weight of what he felt inside, the intimate knowledge that no one else on the planet, excluding his father and Angel, knew. "Lucas's team of Specialists rounded up the last of those involved with Stephens and Leberman at Lincoln Park this morning. Your son is safe. You and Lucas are safe."

She smiled and Cole imagined that it had been some time since she'd smiled in just that way. Without reservation, with profound relief. Her life was her own once more. No more ghosts. No more reading between the lines or looking over her shoulder.

The evil that had haunted the Colby name was gone for good.

"Ms. Parker is well I presume?" he asked, keeping his tone carefully measured, completely professional.

"Mildred is fine," Victoria returned without hesitation. "She asked for some time off to be with her boyfriend."

"Boyfriend?" Cole felt his expression turn amused. So, Victoria wasn't the only indomitable woman at the Colby Agency.

"Yes." Victoria looked pleased. "Dr. Ballard, a long-standing client of this agency. His life and that of his daughter's was endangered a while back. One of my investigators uncovered the scam at his pharmaceuticals corporation. Mildred and Dr. Ballard have been an item ever since."

Another happy ending for the Colby Agency. Cole wondered why it was that real life rarely had so many happy endings. Obviously fate looked kindly upon the Colby Agency. Or perhaps destiny knew that bigger things were in store for the Colby Agency. Certainly the agency's ability to come back from the brink of devastation meant something in the overall scheme of things. Then again, perhaps the past forty-eight hours had softened him somehow, made him start thinking along lines he'd ignored for more than a decade.

If he was lucky, he'd get over it.

Cole Danes didn't rely on fate or destiny. He paved his own way. Just now, however, his destination seemed rather obscure.

He stood, choosing to shirk the sentimental musings. "If you need me for anything else—" he turned to Lucas "—you know where to find me."

Lucas stood, the effort a bit more arduous this morning. Saving his wife's closest confidante had taken a toll on the man. Cole couldn't resist a smile. Some people just didn't know when to quit.

"Thank you again, Mr. Danes."

Cole turned back to Victoria once more before exiting her office. For the first time since meeting her, he realized how uncommonly strong she was. Though silver had invaded her dark hair and decades of pain and suffering marred her dark eyes, neither detracted from her gracious beauty. Victoria Colby-Camp truly was a remarkable woman.

He nodded once then walked away.

He'd long ago surrendered to the idea that there would never be anyone in his life. He could not afford the distraction in his line of work.

The image of an angel flickered before he could block it. Silky white-blond hair, translucent blue eyes. Not even an angel could save a wretched soul such as his.

At the elevator Lucas Camp stabbed the call button and turned back to him. "There were times in the past few days that I had to repress the urge to kill you myself," he said bluntly.

A smiled tugged at one corner of Cole's mouth. "You aren't the first. I doubt you'll be the last."

Lucas didn't look at all surprised by his retort. "In the event that you were asking after the other Ms. Parker—"

"I wasn't," Cole interrupted smoothly.

"I understand," Lucas said knowingly. "Believe me, I do. Just in case you start wondering while en route back to D.C., she's fine. The bullet went straight through soft tissue. No permanent damage. She's taking a few days off to mend and be with her daughter. Otherwise, she's in top form."

Cole stared at the gleaming steel doors refusing to allow Lucas's words to penetrate his defenses. "I'm sure Miss Parker will be fine."

"Me, too," Lucas allowed. "Some young fellow from the hospital assured us that he would take very good care of her. I think he's a doctor or intern or something."

To Cole's relief the doors slid open at that precise instant. "Good day, Lucas." The last thing he wanted was for Lucas to see how his words affected him. Fury mushroomed inside him, unrelenting jealousy. He refused to acknowledge it. Refused to be moved by it.

"You, too, Danes. You, too."

The doors closed, blocking out the view of the grinning man. Cole gritted his teeth. Lucas Camp had no business prying into his life. He'd informed Cole at the warehouse that morning that he knew everything about the coldhearted, relentless Cole Danes. That he knew what he'd done and that he'd better thank his lucky stars that his thirst for revenge hadn't harmed any innocent victims.

And then he'd taken one look at Cole's face as his man Logan brought Angel downstairs and he'd chuckled. Another jolt of fury slashed through Cole. Lucas Camp had known. Damn him, he'd known and there had been nothing Cole could say, for it was undeniably true.

He'd grown attached to Angel Parker. He closed his eyes and let go a weary breath. Damn he was tired. Despite a long, hot shower and a clean bandage on his healing wound, he felt exhausted. He'd gone days without sleep before, that wasn't the real issue. This unfortunate encounter with a bullet was certainly not the first time he'd been shot or otherwise injured. Cole's body had endured many kinds of pain. This nagging hurt felt profoundly foreign to him. Deep and grave. Not a mere wound of the flesh…but closer to the soul.

The wholly amusing part was, Cole considered as he stepped off the elevator into the lobby, all along he'd thought he didn't possess one. Along with a heart, he'd foolishly thought that only the weak lugged around such unnecessary equipment as a soul.

He crossed the parking lot and slid behind the wheel of his SUV. The tightness in his chest would not relent. The knot in his gut refused to relax. He felt empty, hollow.

Perhaps how he felt had more to do with having finished his work than with Angel Parker. He leaned back against the leather headrest. Not likely.

There was one last thing he had to do.

He fished out his cell phone and entered a number from memory. A number he hadn't called in nearly a decade. The fact that he remembered it almost surprised him.

"Hello."

The sound of his father's voice shook Cole in a way he hadn't anticipated. "Hello, Father," he murmured.

"Cole? My God, Son, are you all right?"

Of course his father would think the worst. After all, what would one think when abruptly hearing from someone after eight years?

"It's done. Over. They're all dead." He didn't bother to explain, his father would understand.

The heavy sigh that preceded a lengthy silence proved telling. Relief combined with a hefty dose of trepidation.

"Son, you've got to let this go. Surely you can do that now," his father urged. "You mother and I love you. We only want you to be happy. If sharing your life with us is too painful, we can accept that. What we can't accept is you turning your back on life. Please, please, get on with your life. Put this behind you."

Cole had long awaited this day—had thought numerous times of what he would say to his father, what his father would say to him. He had not expected such simple words to carry such a powerful impact.

"I'll be in touch."

Cole severed the connection, unable to say the rest of what burgeoned in his throat. *I love you, too. I'll be seeing you soon.*

He sat in the quiet of the cold February morning, watched as an unforecast snow started to fall upon the Windy City.

The feeling of emptiness and uncertainty as to what should happen next faded. A kind of understanding took its place.

There was only one thing left for Cole to do.

Chapter Fifteen

Angel kissed her baby's forehead and covered her with a soft pink blanket.

A sigh of deep gratitude eased past her lips.

Her baby was safe at home in her own little bed. Her aunt was unharmed and as vivacious as ever, taking a much-needed vacation with the man she loved. All was as it should be. Life was good again.

Angel reached up and gingerly touched her sore shoulder. She would live.

The evil that had descended upon her life two years ago was gone, obliterated from existence.

By the man she loved.

Ironically, fate had given her that man and then taken him away in the same fell swoop. Cole Danes had walked away without looking back, without even asking if she was okay. But then, he knew she was.

Mildred always said she'd inherited the Parker stubborn streak. Angel would manage. The shoulder

would heal and her heart would, as well. She'd been
down this road once already. A smile slipped across
her lips as she thought of Keith Anderson. He'd
called twice this morning, had rushed to the hospital where she'd received treatment for her shoulder
at the crack of dawn.

He was so cute and undeniably sweet.

But he was not Cole Danes.

She thought of the hard-hearted man who'd
shown up at her house barely three days ago. Of how
he'd threatened her life more than once when all
along he would have risked his own to save hers in
a heartbeat. His relentless, brutal reputation might be
well deserved, but it, apparently, had not extended
to her.

Lucas Camp had warned her when she recovered
from fainting—something she'd never done before
in her life—not to worry about Danes. He was fine.
And, he was gone. The only injuries incurred in the
final shoot-out had been to Clark's men and to
Angel. He didn't mention Cole having asked about
her at all. Only that the mission was complete and
he'd gone.

She closed the door to her baby's room and
slumped against it. Her eyes drifted shut as she attempted without success to rid her mind of those
final images of that evil man. Clark's pilot had shot
at her, hitting his target as well as warning his boss
that someone had rushed up behind him.

Lucky for Angel, dumb beginner's luck at that, she hadn't let the bullet that passed through her shoulder slow her reactions. She'd done exactly as the guy at the pawnshop had told her. *Don't stop shooting until he stops moving.*

Another lucky break had been John Logan, one of Lucas's men. Though, admittedly, luck had not actually been involved. Lucas's men were expert marksmen and had been ordered to move in at the first sign of gunfire. Logan had taken down the pilot, otherwise Angel wouldn't be standing here right now. Logan's decision to shoot the pilot rather than Clark had saved her life, and at the same time allowed Clark the split second necessary to fire his own weapon had Angel not fired first. She hadn't been able to bear the idea of Clark getting away. That's what had sent her running up those roof-access stairs after him. What had driven her to squeeze that trigger when every instinct had screamed at her not to. It wasn't in her nature to hurt anyone, not even a ruthless killer.

But she'd grown weary of not fighting back, of being a victim.

That was another issue she would have to learn to live with. Lucas had told her over and over that she'd only done what had to be done. That, in fact, it may have very well been a shot from Logan that killed the man. She wasn't sure if Lucas merely told her that to make her feel better or if it had actually happened that way. She'd fired several times. The noise from the helicopter and gunfire combined with the shock had likely prevented her from taking in a lot of detail. She might never know.

Some things, she decided, were better left alone.

Clark was dead. His men had been stopped. That's all that mattered.

A knock at her front door jarred her thoughts. Angel tensed instantly, a habit that would surely be hard to break. She heaved a sigh. "Calm down. It isn't the devil."

Determined not to let old fears hang over her like a dark cloud, she pushed off the door and strode into her living room. Surely Keith hadn't made good on his promise and come to her house. She'd told him she needed time alone with her daughter. Somehow she had to get that through his thick skull.

No longer afraid to open the door without looking first, she pasted on a smile and pulled it open wide, a part of her foolishly hoping it might be Cole. Her smile drooped just a little.

"You're supposed to be glad to see me." Keith smiled widely, a huge bouquet of red roses in his arms. "I ditched rounds for this."

"Doctors aren't supposed to ditch rounds," she scolded, helpless not to be flattered by his attention. He truly was adorable and had a terrific professional future ahead of him.

"I'll remember that," he teased. "And, for the record, I'm not actually a doctor yet."

"Come in," she allowed, reaching for the lovely flowers.

COLE PARKED AT THE CURB across the street from Angel's house. For an instant he considered what the hell he was doing here. He should be on that plane back to D.C. There was the final report to do. Though he'd been commissioned by the Colby Agency for this assignment, the case against Stephens and Leberman had remained open with at least three government agencies, including NSA.

That case was now closed.

He supposed he owed it to Angel Parker to check on her one last time before he returned to D.C. A common courtesy. Nothing more. She had been the one to take Clark down, as it were. Taking her statement would be appropriate for his report.

The small sports car parked in front of her house gave him pause. Her vehicle was a four-door sedan, certainly not this shiny red two-seater.

Lucas's words echoed in his brain sending a twist of fury through him. Her social life was none of his business. He knew that and still, the talons of irrational jealousy dug deep. Further proof of how far out of control he had allowed this assignment to get.

But he was back on track now.

There was this one last thing to do and he would be on his way.

Still curious as to whether she had company or not, he pulled out his thermal scanner and checked for himself. One image, then another appeared nearby on the screen, along with a third in a deeper part of the house. He bit back a curse. The second image moved close to the first, too close. Before his brain fully assimilated what that could only mean he was out of the SUV and striding across the street.

He would get this over with and go. Let her get on with her life with…what's his name. The doctor-to-be. He shot a seething look at the sports car as he passed. That sort of vehicle was made for playing the field not settling down. Whatever this man wanted from Angel was not permanent.

A new rush of fury seared through Cole.

He knocked on the door, resisting the urge to kick it down and go in with his weapon drawn.

The door opened and to Cole's supreme annoyance Keith Anderson stood there looking as cocky as ever, as if the next big score were already within his reach.

"Yo, pal, you're looking far better than the last time I saw you." He thrust out his hand.

What the hell kind of doctor started a sentence with yo?

Cole glared at him. "Where is Miss Parker?"

"Oh, ah…" Keith grinned. "Angel is making some

tea." He dropped his hand and stepped back. "Come in. I'm sure there'll be enough for three."

Tea?

Right.

Cole stepped inside, sized up the situation, noting the enormous bouquet of roses dominating the coffee table, then Mr. Anderson's relaxed visage as he closed the door and said, "Have a seat."

As if he were *home* already.

The roar of blood blasting toward Cole's brain blocked all sense of reason. His fingers clenched. He turned his most intimidating gaze on the other man and decided not to make small talk. "Get out," he told him, in a low, deadly tone.

Keith's eyes widened like saucers. "I'll…ah…just be going then."

He was out the door in three seconds flat.

Angel breezed into the room, a tray laden with a porcelain tea set in her hands. Her startled gaze collided with Cole's but she quickly hid her surprise.

"Cole," she said on a rush of breath before looking around the room. "Where's Keith?"

"He had to leave."

She looked confused but then seemed to brush it off. "Okay." She set the tray on the coffee table next to the obscenely mammoth display of roses and took a deep breath.

"What do you want?" she asked when she'd faced him once more. Her voice had changed…hardened.

That was, he admitted woefully, the sixty-four thousand dollar question. What did he want?

Her cheeks flushed with anger and her right foot started to tap against the well-worn hardwood floor. "You disappeared from the warehouse…" She took a moment, visibly composed herself. "Why did you come here?"

Angel wasn't sure what she expected him to say, but she intended to have an explanation. She'd told herself for the past twenty-four hours to forget about him. It was over. He'd done what he came to do, end of story. So what if she'd fallen head over heels. So what if they'd had the most intense sex of her life. It was over. Over, she repeated.

"I wanted to check up on you." He lifted one broad shoulder in a passable shrug. "Make sure you were all right before I leave for D.C."

"You could have waited two minutes in that warehouse to make sure I was all right." She let him have it with both barrels. She hadn't meant to, definitely didn't want to wake Mia. But she just couldn't help it. How dare he!

He stared directly at her with those calm, intimidating eyes looking every bit the dark, mysterious pirate she'd pegged him for from the beginning. She wanted to scream!

"Nice of Mr. Anderson to drop by," he commented dryly.

Was he jealous? That couldn't be. Impossible!

"Yes," she fired back. "Very nice. In fact, we have dinner plans this evening so if you don't mind…" She gestured to the door. "You've come, you've seen, you can go back to where you came from and forget about me."

A line of annoyance, the first she'd seen, appeared between those piercing blue eyes. "Dinner? It's early yet. Surely it won't take so long to prepare for an evening out." A muscle flexed in his lean jaw.

She blinked, her heart thumped. He was jealous! This didn't make sense. As if anything in her life had lately. "What do you want?" she demanded, maintaining her firm stance. She wanted to hear him say it.

He blinked, startled. "I told you. I wanted—"

"I know what you told me," she cut him off. "Now I want the truth." She cocked an eyebrow. "That is if you think I can handle the truth."

He narrowed that laserlike gaze.

"Or maybe you're the one who can't handle the truth."

"What truth?"

Enough. "We made love, Cole," she said bluntly. "I won't ever forget those moments. I won't ever forget you. But I need more than a great climax now and then. I need stability…I need to know what to expect when I wake up in the morning."

Another first. He looked speechless.

He glanced away, set his hands on his hips.

What was the point? He wasn't ready for this. If

he wasn't man enough to admit it, she was damn sure woman enough.

"Just go." She gestured to the door. "Let's not do this to each other."

He started to turn away but stopped. He closed his eyes and drew in a deep breath before opening them once more. And then he asked a question that startled her all over again.

"Where is Mia?"

Startled that he even remembered her daughter's name, she motioned vaguely to the hallway. "She's sleeping. It's her naptime."

Just when she'd thought nothing else that occurred between them could surprise her, he asked, "May I see her?"

She threw her hands up. "Sure." Why not?

Angel led him to her daughter's room, quietly opened the door. Her baby slept with all the innocence and sweetness a child deserved. Angel's thoughts drifted momentarily to Victoria Colby-Camp and her heart wrenched that this had been taken from her. But her son was home now and the devil who'd haunted her was gone for good.

"She's beautiful," Cole murmured. "Just like her mother."

Their gazes locked a moment. Damn her silly emotions. Damn him. A tear streaked down her cheek. She swiped it away, then whispered, "She did get my hair and eyes."

"And your heart I would venture to say."

Angel couldn't do this, couldn't bear it. She stepped back and closed the door. "I'm sorry, but I don't want to wake her." She lifted her gaze to meet his as she spoke. "She has been through an ordeal, as well. I don't want anything else to hurt her."

"Of course."

A moment of awkward silence passed. Why didn't he just go? Didn't he see what this was doing to her.

"Cole—"

He held up a hand to stop her, his expression turning suddenly, stunningly vulnerable. "I…" He hesitated, seemed to search for the right words.

Angel's heart reached out to him as she watched the monumental battle taking place in his eyes, on his face, deep inside him. But she couldn't do this for him. She couldn't be the one. If he'd come here for more than to simply see how she was doing, as she suspected, he had to follow through. He had to give her something concrete to go on.

Like her, a long-lasting nightmare had ended for him. He'd finished what he set out to do, avenging the murder of his brother and the devastation of his family. But there was collateral damage—a term she'd learned in the last seventy-two hours. That, too, she understood. She doubted her life would ever be the same after the events of the past three days, or the past two years really. But she had to move on…get on with her life. He needed to do the same.

"I need you," he said finally. He exhaled a heavy breath then smiled, the features of his handsome face softening in a way she had never seen before. In that moment her lethal pirate transformed into the most handsome man she'd ever laid eyes on. A man who had needs. A man who wanted more.

She didn't know what to say. Now she was the one speechless. Hope bloomed in her chest but she was so afraid to believe…

"I've never done this before, but I want desperately to try."

His confession and vulnerability solidified her tremulous emotions. She reached for his hand, squeezed it, ignoring the little jab of pain that accompanied the move.

"If I've ever met a man in my entire life capable of shaping his own destiny," she assured him, "it's you."

Those deep blue eyes turned agonizingly serious. "Perhaps. There's just one glitch in my plan."

"What's that?"

He tugged her closer. "I need someone to show me how to do this. *I need you.*"

Well, it wasn't "I love you," but Angel knew it was the best he could offer just now.

He glanced toward the bedroom where her daughter slept then back to her. "And your lovely daughter, as well. I need both of you in my life."

"Now that," she allowed, "is a proposition I can live with." Nothing could have pleased her more than his including her daughter. This was a wonderful new beginning.

He cradled her face in those strong hands. "I'd like to properly seal this contract, Miss Parker."

He kissed her, long and deep. And Angel knew that, whatever the future held, they would face it together. As a team and a family. Maybe a soon-to-be larger family. After all, they hadn't used a condom during those wee, frantic hours of the morning. She could hope. With that she planned her own sweet strategy that included a trip a little farther down the hall…in a minute or two. Right now she just wanted to get lost in his kiss.

* * * * *

Don't miss DYING TO PLAY by Debra Webb coming in January 2005.

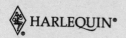

HARLEQUIN®

INTRIGUE®

presents brand-new installments of

HEROES, INC.

from *USA TODAY* bestselling author
Susan Kearney

HIJACKED
HONEYMOON
(HI #808, November 2004)

PROTECTOR S.O.S.
(HI #814, December 2004)

Available at your favorite retail outlet.

HARLEQUIN®
Live the emotion™

www.eHarlequin.com

HIHI2

Like a phantom in the night
comes an exciting promotion from

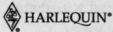 HARLEQUIN®

INTRIGUE

ECLIPSE

GOTHIC ROMANCE

Look for a provocative
gothic-themed thriller each month
by your favorite Intrigue authors!
Once you surrender to the classic
blend of chilling suspense and
electrifying romance in these
gripping page-turners, there will
be no turning back....

Available wherever Harlequin books are sold.

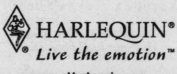 HARLEQUIN®
® *Live the emotion*™

www.eHarlequin.com

HIE3